# DOUBLE-CROSS RANGE

Trouble was the last thing Tyrell needed, but that was just what awaited him in Trueno Valley. He thought a dispute over the owner-ship of the Cross bar A ranch should be resolved in a court of law, but the ranch's ramrod thought otherwise and trouble flared up. Then Tyrell found himself against the Bent Arrow bunch and the lethal, rag-tag 7-Bar outfit. In the background, someone was rigging a lucrative double-cross — while, from Tyrell's own past, crept a deadly shadow . . .

RAY NOLAN

# DOUBLE-CROSS RANGE

*Complete and Unabridged*

LINFORD
*Leicester*

First published in Great Britain in 2002 by
Robert Hale Limited
London

First Linford Edition
published 2004
by arrangement with
Robert Hale Limited
London

British Library CIP Data

Nolan, Ray
  Double-cross range.—Large print ed.—
Linford western library
  1. Western stories
  2. Large type books
  I. Title
  823.9′14 [F]

  ISBN 1–84395–131–2

Published by
F. A. Thorpe (Publishing)
Anstey, Leicestershire

Set by Words & Graphics Ltd.
Anstey, Leicestershire
Printed and bound in Great Britain by
T. J. International Ltd., Padstow, Cornwall

This book is printed on acid-free paper

# 1

Trouble was the last thing Webb Tyrell had any need of. But, wanted or not, it seemed headed his way in the shape of a rider coming hell-for-leather out of the timber, followed by the urgent pounding of other hoofbeats, the echoing crack of gunshots.

'Easy boy,' he whispered when, ears erect, the big roan lifted its head from the water. Slowly he went on building the smoke he'd started, watching as a second rider emerged from between the lofty pines, pause to holster his pistol and wrench a carbine from the saddle boot. 'Easy,' he said again when the horse pawed the muddy ground, nickering irritably.

The horsemen were still a distance from where he'd stopped to let the gelding drink, atop a timber-ridged rise that angled sharply down to the water

1

hole, too far to see their faces as more than blurs of color. He watched the second rider lift and level the carbine, heard it bark twice and saw the first, already well down the slope, rise up in his stirrups before toppling from the saddle.

The one who'd done the shooting started cautiously down, gun held at ready against his hip. Tyrell ditched the unlighted quirly, reaching for his Colt as he dismounted, knowing the distance was too great for anything but a warning shot, but aware and disliking the fact that the fallen rider was about to be assured of a straight-away ticket to hell. Or wherever else he might be destined.

Until then the second horseman had been too focused on bringing down his quarry to have noticed the man and his horse paused at the seep. Conscious of him now, he pulled rein and swung the carbine around. In doing so, he put the sun behind him, obscuring his image even more.

Tyrell slapped the gelding's glistening rump. 'Go!' he muttered, bringing up his own weapon at the same time as the rider came charging downslope, firing as he dug in spurs.

Lead buzzing inches above his head, Tyrell hit the ground, squeezing trigger as he went, rolling to the left, coming up on his elbows, waiting until his attacker was a little closer before snapping off two more shots. There had been no time to aim, yet almost miraculously, he saw the long gun fly from his would-be killer's grasp, saw him abruptly tighten rein and jerk the gray he straddled into a tight turn, high-tailing it back to the protection of the pine.

Cursing softly, Tyrell got back to his feet, called to the roan. With ears still stiffly erect, it came to him. 'Don't ask me,' he said softly, in the manner of a man who'd grown accustomed to talking to the only living thing to which he was close.

On the way to the fallen rider, he

3

collected the gun that had been dropped, wasting no time examining it.

There were two bullet holes in his back. The first, low down and to the right, would have crippled him; the second, larger and higher and to the left, had finished him. Or just about. Tyrell got down on his haunches and turned him over. He was young, probably in his mid-twenties. A good-looking kid. His eyes opened, staring. The kid blinked twice, swallowed hard. 'Double-crossing bast — ' The rest was stifled by a spasm that stiffened his body, stretched his eyes wide a moment before the lids dropped.

Tyrell turned to look back at the timber, but there was no sign or sound of anyone up there now. He pushed upright, picked up the discarded Winchester from where he'd let it drop, turning it carefully over in his hands before shunting another frowning glance up the slope.

No name or any other identifying mark had been engraved into the butt plate, or anywhere else on the weapon.

A distance away, beyond the water hole where the ground began another upward swing, he spotted the dead man's horse, motionless and staring back at him. For a while he stood undecided, knowing he could not leave the boy where he'd fallen, nor could he simply bury him. He shook his head. For a man not wanting trouble, he'd inherited a fistful in one hell of a hurry.

With the body roped across the saddle of the nervous dun, Tyrell lifted himself back into leather. The brand the dead man's horse carried resembled a mission bell-tower, a small cross crowning a rounded letter A. But he was a man in a strange country, with no idea whether he was already on Cross bar A range, or, if he was, in which direction he'd find its headquarters. Nor had he any notion where the nearest town might be.

An hour's easy riding took him deeper into the valley, where small knots of cattle grazed, wearing the same brand as the led horse, but no nearer to any type of settlement. He squinted up at the sun, figured the time to be at least a couple of hours before noon, and started the roan moving again, toward a rocky outcropping that narrowed the trail he followed. He was well in between the rocks when a voice snapped:

'Throw 'em high and keep 'em stiff!'

Tyrell swore under his breath, but did as ordered, not knowing how many were at his back.

'Now — using your left hand — very careful-like, lift that iron you're packing and let it drop. One mistake and I introduce you to eternity!'

Again Tyrell chose not to argue.

From behind came the scraping of boots upon hard ground, and then someone was standing a short distance behind him, telling him to dismount. In doing so he was able to turn, to see who had brought him to a halt. A tall drink of water of at least thirty, with light-blue eyes and a face which was handsome in a rough-hewn way. The gun he fisted was held steady and confidently, his expression set hard and cold, inviting the slightest of wrong moves.

'You better have a damn fine reason for this,' he said gratingly. 'A real damn fine reason. This here's young Henkel's pony, and less'n my eyes have gone back on me ... ' He took another forward step, flicked a quick, closer look at the body the dun carried, then swung his gaze sharply back to Tyrell, a hoarse curse ripping from his throat, the gun lifting, trigger-finger tightening dangerously. 'Damn you! It *is* him! That's Roy you got there!'

Tyrell shrugged. 'Have to take your word for it. We never had time for introductions.'

The other motioned curtly. 'Keep goin'.'

Briefly Tyrell told him how he came to be toting the body. When he finished, the tall one was scowling.

'I'm supposed to swallow that?'

A lean-bodied man, wide-shouldered, and as tall as the one pointing the gun, hollow-cheeked face seared by many suns, with eyes dark and seemingly haunted by events of a past kept well hidden, Tyrell pulled himself upright.

'Believe what you like,' he answered quietly. 'But if I'd killed him, you think I'd be toting him along behind me?' His head jerked towards the dun. 'You'll find a 30-30 back there with him. Belongs to the one who did the shooting.'

The answer to his question received a long moment's consideration. 'You got a name?'

Tyrell told him.

'And you're on Cross bar A, doing what?'

'Didn't know I was. Not till running into this. Passing through is all I had in mind.'

'To where?'

Again Tyrell shrugged. 'No place — any place.'

For a while they studied each other

in silence. Then the one holding the gun said, 'This could cost me, but . . . ' he lowered the weapon. 'Name's Stretch Norton. That there's — *was* — Roy Henkel, also of Cross bar A.'

Tyrell glanced at the sky. 'Might be an idea we got him someplace where he'll keep a little better.'

# 2

The sun was almost directly overhead when they reached Cross bar A headquarters, an impressive array of buildings, well constructed and intelligently positioned amid tall shade trees. Yet, faint though they were, signs of neglect, of painting and repairs overdue, were starting to show.

They came in quietly, Stretch Norton setting the example, and were met near the huge barn by a bow-legged oldster, whiskered and minus most of his teeth. Narrowed eyes fastened hard upon Tyrell when Norton made the introduction, taking their sweet time in judgment, making note of the flat-crowned black hat, gray shirt, and dark whipcord pants, gaze lingering a while longer on the shell-belt and holster. No run-of-the mill rangeman this, Denver Crowley concluded. But it was a glimmer of some deeply concealed quality found in the man's face that held his attention, that allowed his shoulders to relax when giving Norton a quick nod.

'Let's get him into the barn,' he said, removing his battered hat to run fingers through hair long enough to cover his ears. 'Don't want Miz Dana to see him like that.'

'Bit late,' Stretch muttered, looking beyond him, toward the big house.

Tyrell's eyes were already upon the girl who'd come silently on to the gallery, moving to the wooden steps, there to stand for a long moment watching them. Now she was crossing the yard, walking with determination if not haste. A fairly tall, narrow-waisted girl with dark hair, gathered at the back of her neck. Only when coming to a stop at the old man's side was he able to fully appreciate either her youth or the splendour of figure and features. Not beautiful, but striking in a manner that would hold a man's attention longer than any gaudy almanac illustration.

In a voice forced to calmness she said, 'It's Roy, isn't it?'

''Fraid so,' Denver sighed. 'This's the feller seen it happen. Name's Tyrell — Webb Tyrell.' To Tyrell he said, 'This's the boss lady, Miz Dana Lane. Tell her what you jes' told me.'

His hat already removed, Tyrell dipped his head in acknowledgment. With a minimum of words he repeated his story.

'I appreciate you bringing him in,' she said when he'd finished, unable to fully conceal the mist in her eyes, the struggle to keep her voice under control. 'Roy was more than just a very good hand. Along with Denver and Stretch . . . he was one of the most loyal men I've known.' She squared her shoulders, bringing the pale-blue shirt she wore taut across full breasts. 'I thank you, Mr Tyrell, and offer you the hospitality of Cross bar A. I only wish you'd been able to get a better look at the one who — who did this.'

Denver, still holding the Winchester used to kill the boy, gave it another fast and needless scrutiny.

'Only fresh marks I can see're up here close to the magazine. Either one of your slugs knocked it outa his hands, or you winged the sunnuva — the coyote. Somethin' had to make him drop it.'

Receiving no comment from Tyrell, the girl placed a hand gently upon Denver's narrow shoulder.

'We'll bury Roy here on the ranch. But first we'll take him into town so that he — can be properly prepared.'

'And let the marshal know what's happened,' Denver growled with mild derision. 'Not that I 'spect it'll do a whole lotta good, but I guess we better.' He shoved the carbine at Stretch. 'I'll get things organized.'

Her hand returned briefly to his shoulder. 'No, Denver. Stretch can take me. You stay here, watch over things — see that Mr Tyrell gets fed, his horse taken care of.' Her dark eyes lifted back to Tyrell. 'You're very welcome to stay overnight. And I thank you again.' She turned to Norton. 'Stretch, if — if you'll get Roy a change of clothes . . . ' The back of her hand brushed quickly at her eyes. 'I'll be ready in a few minutes.' Face rigid, she started back to the house.

Norton's eyes followed her, and though taking care not to make it obvious, his slight change of expression revealed much of his regard for the girl.

'You heard the lady,' Denver said. 'And I second the invite. You look like you could use a bellyful of grub.'

Tyrell pulled his gaze away from Norton, now headed for the buildings to the left of the house.

'And someone your marshal might want to question?'

The old man scratched his chin. 'There's that.'

'He's got jurisdiction out here?'

'Nope. But, with a sheriff that sits nice an' comfy up at the county seat, sendin' down a deputy only when he's got nothin' better to do . . . ' He left the rest for Tyrell to figure.

A while after Dana Lane and Norton had taken off in the buckboard carrying the body of the young Cross bar A hand, Tyrell and Denver Crowley were parked on a bench near the cookshack, in the shade of a massive oak. The old man, he'd noticed, carried a gun, even here at their home base. He took another drag on the recently-lit ciga-rette. 'Nice set-up you got here.'

Denver nodded somberly, offering nothing in return.

Tyrell's gaze shifted to the bunk-house, large enough to accommodate a dozen or more.

'Must have a fair size riding crew.'

'Used to. You already met all that's left.' Chewing thoughtfully, Denver paused to squint at Tyrell, as if trying to make up his mind about something. A dark stream of tobacco juice left his mouth to splatter in the yard, and when speaking again, anger thickened his voice. 'Last three months, ever since Nat Anderson's been dead, we been havin' nothin' but trouble. Not that we never had none before. Only now it's gotten to be real heavy. Hands scared off, cattle lifted . . . every danged thing to make a body want to cash it all in. Way it stands now, with young Roy gone, there's jes' me an' Stretch left to try and hold things together.'

Nat Anderson, according to what Crowley had already told, had been the man who'd built Cross bar A, who'd willed everything to his niece.

'Ain't a blood relative,' he'd explained, 'but maybe closer'n any of that kind could ever be. Her pa was a close friend to Nat. Fourteen years back, both her folks got killed in some kinda freak accident, and Nat took her in. Jes' goin' on twelve, she was, skinny and frightened.' His voice softened. 'Been like a daughter to him, she has.' Again there was a sort of pause used to weigh up the intelligence of saying more. 'Place should've already been

16

hers. 'Cept that, jes' before it could happen there was' — he spat again, scornfully — 'what you might call a legal complication.'

Tyrell took another drag on the cigarette before asking: 'Any particular reason for your troubles?'

'Couple of possibles, but no proof.' For a while Denver was silent. Then, pointing in an easterly direction, he said, 'Morg Farraday's got his Bent Arrow spread down that-away. Two — three years ago he started tryin' to get ol' Nat to sell. Then he gave up. Which's about when the trouble got started. Little things at first, but they began buildin' up kinda fast.'

Tyrell dropped the cigarette butt, heeling it into the earth.

'Rustling?'

Again Denver hesitated. 'Yeah, but somehow I don't see Farraday that way involved. Neither could Nat, even though, long ago — before Miz Dana came along — from bein' good friends, they was suddenly hatin' each other's guts. Farraday's as ornery as ever they was made, but not so stupid as to dirty his hands with stolen beef.' He shook his head, rope-scarred fingers worrying his beard. 'Nope, not Bent Arrow. We been losin' stock, small bunches that disappear from time to time, but if anybody's been swingin' sticky loops, I'll put my money on that scurvey 7 bar lot.'

Sensing rather than recognizing Tyrell's frowned question, he pointed again, this time west, where rocky hills rose in high green-and-tan smudges again a backdrop of blue.

'Hardcase name of Jelnick's got a ragtag spread back there someplace. Got hisself two riders, both cut from the same hide.' Denver's voice grew gradually softer as he went on squinting thoughtfully in the direction he'd pointed. ''Bout a half-hour's ride from where you reckon you saw young Roy get hisself shot . . . Which's somethin' to ponder.' He stood up, using both hands to massage the small of his back while looking down at Tyrell. 'What'd it take to get you ridin' for us?'

Tyrell also rose. 'Hadn't figured on taking any job. Not just yet.'

Denver's eyes dropped to the holster thonged down above the younger man's knee. 'Pity.'

An almost imperceptible tightening came to Tyrell's jaw. But he said nothing, watching instead a distant rise of dust heralding incoming riders.

'Looks like company on the way.'

Slowly, Denver turned, stared, and spat again. 'Comin' from Farraday's end of the valley,' he muttered. 'Wonder what the hell's bitin' at his butt now . . . ?'

# 3

There were three of them, the one in the middle, chunky, astride a handsome dappled white. Disregarding the two men in the ranch yard, they rode directly to the house.

'Want somethin'?' Denver called.

Morgan Farraday twisted slowly around. A ruddy-faced, middle-aged man with a short spade beard and deep-set eyes that glared back in disdainful silence. He started to dismount.

Denver waited until he was on the ground. 'Wouldn't waste time goin' any further. Ain't nobody home.'

'Where is she?' the one who'd rode at Farraday's right snapped. Bigger, heavier, thick-thighed and sullen-faced, he boasted the same ruddy complexion as Farraday.

'None of your — ' Denver started to

growl, then let a slow smile cut it short. 'Then again . . . might jes' be. Some yellow-bellied backshooter this mornin' killed Roy Henkel. Miz Dana's taken him to be made ready for a decent buryin'.' From the side of his mouth he whispered to Tyrell: 'Roley Farraday. Mean bastard. Skinny one's called Idaho Smith. Watch him.'

Tyrell had already been doing just that.

With a quiet curse Morgan Farraday hauled himself back aboard the white, turning it to cross the yard. The others fell in at his sides. When they stopped he scowled at Tyrell.

'Who're you?'

Tyrell answered with a small frown.

'You deaf?' the younger Farraday growled. 'My father asked a question!'

'And I'm wondering what would make it his business.'

The third rider, a thin moustache emphasizing the fullness of his upper lip, sat silent, smiling wryly. Tyrell paid him no attention, his eyes on the man who had left his saddle.

'My father asked a question,' Roley Farraday repeated, heavy shoulders bunching as he came forward.

Tyrell made no reply, waiting until Farraday's right leg swung into the third long step that would bring him up close. Then, straightening, he took an almost casual kick at the descending boot, swiping the man's heavy leg out from under him.

Farraday went down hard, an involuntary curse erupting from his lungs.

'Hold it!' Tyrell heard a voice bark, and from the corner of an eye saw Denver move forward, gun fisted, and tilted upward. He flicked a look at the two mounted men and saw the lanky one's hand freeze, then drop away from his holster.

Tyrell put his gaze on Morgan Farraday. 'Want to teach him a little patience, some manners.'

Cursing loudly, Roley Farraday pushed himself up from the ground, murder in distended eyes as he swung toward Tyrell.

'Roland!' his father's voice thundered, stopping him in his tracks. 'Enough! That's not what we're here for!'

Roley stood momentarily undecided, then bent to pick up his hat from where it had fallen. 'We're not through,' he grated, the rage within him showing no sign of abating.

Gun still pointed, Denver turned to Morgan Farraday. 'What exactly was it you wanted?'

At first it looked as if Farraday would remain frozen-faced and clammed up. But, waiting until his son was again mounted, he said, 'Tell her I'm still waiting for an answer.'

'Be a long wait,' returned Denver. 'Miz Dana's of no mind to sell.'

'We'll see.' Farraday lifted reins. 'She'll find running a ranch is no job for a girl. She'll sell, but when she does, it may not be at the price I'm presently offering.'

The last of the trio to turn away was the man called Idaho Smith. Before doing so, he raised a finger to his hat-brim in a farewell salute. 'Be seeing you,' he said quietly, smiling thinly, knowingly, at Tyrell.

* * *

Ben Paulson sat on the edge of his flat-top desk, listening without interruption while Dana Lane talked, aware that the way he felt about her, how he'd felt about her ever since taking up the post of town marshal, was the cause of his present discomfort. In the two years he'd been in Cradlestone he'd not been of any worthwhile assistance to either her or her uncle, a fact which made it even more difficult to confess his feelings. He rose now, running sturdy fingers through thick, wavy black hair, knowing that once again he'd be of little help.

'This Tyrell — you think he was telling the truth?'

24

Frowning a little, Dana lifted herself from the wooden chair.

'I've no reason not to. Why else would he go to the trouble of bringing Roy's body back to the ranch?'

'I don't know.' Paulson shrugged helplessly. 'So much has been happening out there . . . '

'Like Uncle Nat's death,' she added quietly.

Paulson sighed softly. At thirty, his clean-shaven face showed few lines, still retained traces of boyish good looks. In his boots he stood only fractionally taller than the girl before him, another awareness he did not much enjoy. He said, 'Dana . . . there's never been any proof, no evidence at all to — '

'Of course there hasn't,' she returned with some acrimony. 'Whoever engineered his death was far too clever for that. But I'll never be convinced that Uncle Nat would allow a horse to throw him — especially the one he was riding that day. He was far too good a rider.' She turned to point at the

Winchester lying on the desk, the one Tyrell had brought in with Roy Henkel's body. 'Do you think there'll be any chance of tracing it to its owner?'

Paulson emitted another small sigh. 'Doubt it. There are hundreds of guns like that around. Nothing special about that one to tell us anything.'

Dana adjusted the cream-colored Stetson to a slightly firmer position on her head.

'All right, Ben,' she said, tone easing. 'I realize all of this is out of your jurisdiction. I know you can't — '

'Darnit, Dana,' he cut in, 'you know I've tried. But you have to understand my position. There's never been proof of anything, nothing to get a handle on — not the rustling, not the reason for your crew drifting.' He drew a deeper breath, let it out slowly, bringing a sag to his shoulders. 'I've telegraphed the county sheriff, requesting that he send down a deputy. But again, without proof . . . '

'I'm sorry,' she said. 'It's just that

conditions are becoming difficult. I've barely any crew left and my money's about run out . . . '

'Taking that fancy-pants lawyer a long time to get things settled, isn't it?' Paulson frowned. 'Thought your uncle's will was cut and dried — that you got everything?'

'It's not his fault, Ben. There — there are certain matters that first need to be — settled.' She paused, as if wanting to tell him more, but instead made a half-turn to the door. 'I'm on my way to see him now. Hopefully he'll have better news for me.'

★   ★   ★

Vance Beresford, the only lawyer in Cradlestone, had upstairs offices in the same brick building as the bank. A tall man, thick from neck to knees, with little fat contributing to his weight. A distinguished-looking man of at least forty, graying at the temples, with eyes that seemed a bit oversize, showing too much white. He stood up when the girl entered, straightening his gray frock-coat.

'Dana! I'm so glad you came.' Hurrying around the desk he held one of the two upholstered chairs, inviting her to be seated.

'I had to,' she said, waiting until he was settled back in his swivel chair before telling him about the death of the young ranch hand.

Beresford shook his head, muttering something sympathetic.

'I also needed to see you,' she went on before he could say more, looking straight into a face which had lost its smile. 'I need to have some money, and until Cross bar A is legally mine, the bank claims to be unable to advance anything from my uncle's account. Nor lend me a dollar without collateral.'

'Dana, I thought you understood. As your uncle's executor, from that account I'm permitted to pay all the operating expenses of the ranch — just as I have been doing, and will continue doing until the estate is finally — '

'I know,' she answered quickly. 'But there are other things needed, and I've just about used up every penny of my own.'

A concerned expression clouding his broad face, Beresford leaned back. 'There is nothing personal in the bank's attitude, I assure you. It's simply standard business practice. But, in the meantime . . . I'm sure I could lend you whatever you need.'

She shook her head. 'I appreciate that, but I'd rather not.' A small, slightly cynical smile moved her mouth. 'You don't think perhaps Morgan Farraday used a little influence? He's been wanting Cross bar A for a long time.'

'Unfortunately, I'm in no position to comment on Farraday's tactics — though his interest in the ranch is no secret. As you know, he's tried to have me persuade you to sell.' Beresford's fingers entwined themselves across his middle. 'He knows nothing, of course, about our problem — about the letter received from the woman claiming to have been your uncle's wife.'

For a while Dana was silent.

'I asked Denver about her,' she said at last. 'But the little I did get had to be dragged out of him.' Her eyes dropped to the level of the desk. 'I've always known Uncle Nat had been married, but he — he never talked about it.'

'He was.' Beresford nodded solemnly. 'I've been through all the papers — everything Edward Armstrong had on file before I took over his practice. Unfortunately, nowhere could I find any record of a divorce — *or* a death.' Dana started to say something, but he got in first. 'There's more . . . unfortunately. Amongst Armstrong's papers I found two more of the woman's letters — all in the same handwriting, each signed 'Mrs Florence Anderson'.'

Face growing pallid, the girl waited for the rest.

'It appears,' he added slowly, 'that on various occasions she'd found herself in difficulties and written to Armstrong, hoping he could solicit financial assistance from your uncle. According to those letters, she'd previously written directly to him, but he'd ignored all her pleas — despite her situation.'

Dana's head lifted a little. 'Then he must have had a reason, because Uncle Nat was one of the kindest men who ever lived.' She stood up, making a small adjustment to the wide belt of the corduroy split skirt she was wearing. 'What happens next?'

Rolling back his chair, the lawyer rose and came slowly around the desk. 'That's why I was glad you came — why I wanted to see you.' He took a deep breath, exhaling wearily. 'She'll be arriving on Friday's stage. We'll know more about how we stand then.' He tarried again, countenance growing grim. 'There's one other thing you need to keep in mind, Dana. If her claim concerning her son can be substantiated — if she can prove he is your uncle's issue — we might have a serious problem.'

'How serious?' she asked, sensing still more bad news.

'Very. I took the liberty of discussing such a situation with Judge Thackery, and he's of the opinion that — well, there's a good chance a court could accept him as the rightful heir to your uncle's entire estate.'

# 4

It was close to sunset before Stretch and Dana arrived back at Cross bar A, and not much later when Webb Tyrell and the remnants of her crew were having supper in the dining-room of the main house instead of the galley. Loneliness, or perhaps no more than a need of association and belonging had, after most of her riders drifted, stirred Dana Lane to adjust the old order.

Through eating, they listened attentively while she informed them about the woman named Flo, of her imminent arrival.

'Kinda sudden, ain't it?' Denver queried, an eyebrow suspiciously atilt. 'Friday's jes' two days off.'

'I know. Even Mr Beresford only learned about it when receiving her telegram this morning.' To Tyrell she said, 'Vance Beresford's the lawyer

33

who's handled all my uncle's affairs these past years.'

For a while there was an awkward silence at the long table. Denver, knowing she was looking at him, tried to avoid her eyes.

'What happened between her and Uncle Nat, Denver?'

As long as he could, he held his silence.

'Miz Dana, it ain't proper I talk about what ain't none of my business.'

Very carefully, Tyrell pushed back his chair and stood up. 'If you'll excuse me, I could use a smoke.'

Immediately Stretch Norton, who'd been riding for the brand only three years, did likewise. 'Same here.'

A touch of sadness swept through Dana's smile. 'Unless you really mean that, there's no need for either of you to leave. After Friday, I imagine the entire county will know what's happening.'

'It's still family business,' Tyrell muttered.

'Nevertheless, there's no need for

either you or Stretch to leave. You're new to Cross bar A, Mr Tyrell, but rightly or wrongly, I believe there's a reason for you riding into our lives.' Her eyes met his, and held. 'Denver's told me what happened when Morgan Farraday was here this afternoon. Please' — she made a small hand-gesture, her glance softening when it moved to Stretch — 'sit down. Both of you.'

'You heard,' Denver grunted. 'Anchor yourself.'

Their discomfort apparent, both men resumed their seats. Already Tyrell had come to a few pleasant conclusions concerning the girl, and now other characteristics were emerging that had him wishing the trails he'd left behind had contained far fewer shadows.

'As I have no need to tell you,' she said hesitantly, after a moment of tomblike silence, 'for the past three months all of Cross bar A's running expenses have been paid through Mr Beresford's office, and until — one way or another — everything has been settled, this will continue. But I have had other expenses, and to meet them I've been drawing on the few dollars I've owned. Come the end of the month, however, there'll be nothing left.' Gently she bit down on her lower lip before going on. 'In fact, Cross bar A could very soon have a new owner.'

Denver's head jerked up. 'What's that s'posed to mean?'

'Simply that if the woman claiming to be Uncle Nat's widow succeeds with her action, everything will become hers, or her — '

'The hell it will!' Denver exploded.

Dark eyes were misted when she turned to the oldster who, along with her Uncle Nat, had always been there to guide her, teach her ... so many times, to comfort and encourage.

'I'm afraid,' she said, 'there's a good chance that it will.'

'Dagnabbit, that jes' wouldn't be right! Nohow!' Denver growled emphatically.

'She can't do that! She ain't got no right!'

'Unfortunately, according to Mr Beresford — and Judge Thackery, whom he consulted on the matter — if her credentials are in order, she has every right. And every chance of succeeding.'

'What do they know?' the old man growled, then became very quiet, so much so that the thoughts tumbling about in his head were almost audible. Eyes firmly upon his clean-scoured plate, he asked, 'How'd she find out Nat was dead anyway?'

'According to one of her letters to Mr Beresford, a friend passed along the news. Presumably someone in Cradlestone who has always known how to contact her.'

'Someone,' Stretch put in hesitantly, 'who maybe had little liking for your uncle. Maybe not a whole lot more for you . . .'

'Farraday!' Denver spat out the name contemptuously.

'No,' Dana responded with a quick headshake. 'If he knew her, and what she'd intended, he'd never have been out here as late as today, still trying to get me to sell. No, I don't think it was him.'

'Then who?'

'I've no idea, but for the moment it doesn't matter.' Another long moment's silence, then, speaking directly to Denver Crowley, she said, 'You see, she won't be arriving alone. She'll be bringing her son with her.'

Denver's chair jerked backward. 'Her what?'

Dana repeated what she'd said.

The old man's head started a slow wagging. 'If there's that, then I'll be double-danged and hung out to dry! There was never no talk about — about no such thing when she left! If there was, Nat would never've turned her loose, no matter what! No, dagnabbit, I don't believe it! Flo would've — would've — Nah,' he said, cutting it short, head again shaking. 'I don't believe it!'

The silence that descended upon the room was heavy and long. Denver broke it by thumping the table. 'No, sirree! No way is she goin' to get away with it. She's no damn good, that woman! Never was!' His mouth was still working, but, realizing the effect his outburst had caused, he shut it. Roughly massaging his whiskered chin, he muttered, 'Sorry. Had no call to do that. Jes' that — jes' that I figure Nat realized he'd made a whoppin' big mistake, hitchin' up with her. Met her while up in Leadville, negotiatin' to supply beef to the mines. Time he come back, she was his wife.'

Many times had Tyrell experienced uncomfortable situations, but the one in which he found himself now was the kind that had him squirming. Yet, though possessed with a dislike of gossip, he found himself listening because it involved Dana Lane's welfare, her future. Somehow that had become important to him.

'She broke Nat's heart,' Denver was saying. 'Never was a proper wife — never gave a hoot about Cross bar A. Except for what it could give her. Money went like water through her hands, an' she had no interest in tryin' to keep a proper home for Nat.' He ran the back of his hand across his mouth, as if trying to wipe away dirt that had spilled through his lips. 'They had fights, her and Nat. Lots of 'em. But this I can tell you straight: your uncle was too much of a gentleman to ever lay a hand on her.'

Gnarled fingers brushed through his long gray thatch. 'Somethin' happened — somethin' I ain't prepared to discuss — that ended it. Nat gave her money, seen she was on a stage out of the territory, and that was it — last we ever seen of her.' Bitterness tightened the old ramrod's face. 'She left with money an' better clothes than she come with, an' — well, let's jes' say she seemed glad to be shaking off the dust of this place.' His gaze lifted. 'Then you come

along, and it was like a new dawnin' in
ol' Nat's life. I never seen him happier,
an' I swear before all the saints, I never
heard him talk no more about that
woman.'

★  ★  ★

Tyrell was sitting in the dark, on the
bench under the giant oak, when he
heard quiet footsteps. Turning, he saw
the shadowy form of the girl approaching. He stood, dropped the cigarette
he'd been smoking, and stepped on it.

'Am I intruding?' she asked.

'Far from it.'

Clasping hands behind her back, she
stared into the night, seeing things only
she could see.

'I'd hate to have to leave here.'

'Probably never come to that,' he
said, conscious of a gentle fragrance
that had not been there before her
arrival.

She sighed softly. 'I'm trying to hold
on to that hope, but it's becoming

difficult. If Uncle Nat had a son, I guess he'd be more entitled to . . . '

'That's something still to be decided, isn't it?'

Instead of answering, she turned to face him. 'I'll also be sorry to see you leave. But then, the way things are shaping, there'd be no sense in you staying, would there?'

'I'll be around,' he murmured.

'Oh . . . ? I thought Denver said you were drifting on . . . '

'Be hanging around town for a while.' He dragged the sack of Bull Durham from a shirt-pocket. 'Be there, ever you should have need of me.'

'Thank you.' On his arm came the feather touch of her fingers. 'Good-night,' she whispered, and then she was gone.

He had a fresh cigarette burning when Denver showed himself.

'No reason you can't dump your gear here,' he muttered.

'How long you been skulking back there, old-timer?'

'Long enough.' Denver sat down next to him. 'Ask you somethin' personal?'

Tyrell shrugged.

'You runnin' from somethin'?'

Studying the glowing tip of the cigarette, Tyrell shrugged. Sometime during the past three weeks he'd begun to feel as if a shadow trailed behind him. He'd tried dismissing it as imagination, but the feeling refused to go away.

'I don't know, Denver,' he said. 'I don't know. Maybe we're all running from something.'

# 5

He'd said nothing to Denver or anyone else, but, next morning, once out of sight of the ranch, he turned westward. Letting the roan fall into a steady, unhurried lope, he headed to where he'd seen a bullet tip Roy Henkel out of the saddle.

With more time to focus upon his surroundings, the further he back-tracked the greater became his appreciation of Farraday's desire to possess this range. Grass was good and plentiful. So was water, supplied by what appeared to be spring-fed holes that would more than take year-round care of a truly good-size herd. Anderson had either chosen well or been blessed with an excess of good fortune when electing to settle in this section of the valley.

He paused only briefly when arriving

at the place where Henkel had drawn his last breath, then started upslope, toward the timber. About a half-mile beyond, the ground began to get rough and inhospitable as it crept closer to the hills. He kept riding at the same easy pace, the sun's touch growing warmer. And the signs were there, but you had to look for them. Signs that spoke of cattle and horses.

He almost missed it because it veered suddenly off to the right, to where brush had thickened, almost throttling the old and seldom-used trail. He stopped for a moment, studying the ground without finding any need to leave the saddle. Then he pushed through the dense growth, following the narrow trace down into a small, rock-strewn pocket. There, still defying the elements, stood the remains of an ancient shack, its roof long gone, weeds grown as high as the single, glassless window.

Tyrell shuttled a slow, scrutinizing glance around the place. A long time ago someone had probably believed the hills held riches. Now tangled, spiky shrub obliterated whatever attempts had been made to uncover them. The place had a deserted, totally forsaken appearance. Except for the cigarette butts and horse apples discarded within a few feet of the derelict shack.

He got down to examine them. The ground itself was too hard to offer much more than turned-over stones and scuffed earth, hinting that more than one rider had stopped here at various times. The last, according to two of the butts and the freshest of the droppings, probably no more than a day ago.

For a while he stood perfectly still, committing the scene to memory, and again there was the eerie sensation of someone or something unseen staring at his back. He went on listening, glance roving the rocky walls that surrounded him, and found nothing. Finally he climbed back into leather, pointing the roan out of the hollow, and back along the narrow trail.

Within just a short while he found a resumption of the cattle tracks, still pointing westward, following the base of the hills. He remembered that Denver had told him the 7-Bar was located somewhere up here. He kept going, watching the ground spill out slowly in front of him. Another half-hour later the sun-baked trail abruptly intercepted another, a broader, but fainter one over which many hoofs had tramped.

He was moving between the foothills, headed for still higher ground, when it happened. All around him rose a sudden sound of smothered thunder that jerked the roan to a startled halt. He twisted about, listening, but the terrain made it impossible to detect the source. The horse nickered, shifted warily. Then, after no more than a minute, as abruptly as it had started, the strange rumbling was gone.

He recalled Denver's explanation, when being told the name of the place where yesterday he had found himself. Somewhere in the forgotten past, he'd opined, probably because of the manner in which the backdrop of hills echoed and amplified the sound of thunder — a sound not heard much these days — some Spanish tongue had been inspired to christen the place Trueno Valley. Thunder Valley. Tyrell lifted his gaze to the sky, and shrugged. The racket had sounded and felt more like an earth tremor.

* * *

He came upon the ranch much sooner than he'd expected, a place of a few miserable gray-weathered, unpainted buildings, planted upon stark, baked earth, where even the few cottonwoods seemed to be held up by no more than desperation. Touching heels to the roan, he started slowly across the hard-packed yard to where a three-man reception committee had come out from the house.

Stepping to the fore, the tallest, a man with a way to go before touching thirty, pale coppery hair poking out from under a coffee-colored hat, hooked thumbs into his gunbelt, waiting until the intruder stopped.

'Looking for something?' Reddish beard-stubble smudged a face that would never readily accept sun and wind.

'This your place?'

'I asked was you lookin' for something.'

His stance, the way he wore his gun — Tyrell had seen it all before, on others who figured they had something to prove. He looked beyond him to the other two who stayed closer to the house. One was running to fat, a greasy, dark-bearded number. The third, weasel-faced and small of frame, with shifty, nervous eyes.

'Your name Jelnick?' he asked the bearded man who, despite his appearance, carried an air of authority.

'What's it to you?' The man took

another forward step, hands akimbo, one convenient to his gun. 'And like you already been asked — you looking for something?'

'Uh-huh. Cross bar A beef. Found tracks suggesting a few head may've found their way up here.'

His expression didn't change, but the back of the weasel-faced one appeared to tighten up.

'That some kind of accusation, pilgrim?'

'No . . . ' Tyrell drawled. 'Not this time. But in case Cross bar A get to lose any more stock . . . Well, now, this could be the first place I reckon I'd come looking.'

The redhead spat out a raw curse, right hand leaping, hovering impatiently over the butt of his gun.

'Mister, nobody rides in here and makes that kinda talk! You got exactly five seconds to suck wind — or lose one of your ears!' He started counting.

'Johnny — ' The bearded one's head jerked to the left, but before he could manage another word the carrot-top had finished his count, was making a rapid swipe at his holster.

The gun was clear, lifting, when what felt like a bolt of lightning streaked across the top of his wrist. The gun spun from his fingers at the same time as he heard the shot. He reeled backward, staring with disbelief at the bloody furrow.

Hard and cold, Tyrell's voice reached at him. 'Ever you try that again, boy, it'll be your head.'

The one who'd so far done most of the talking came forward, face dark with fury but careful to keep his hands in sight. 'Who the hell d'you think you are, coming up here, making wild charges — shooting up my pardners?'

'Name's Tyrell. And you'd be?'

'Frank Jelnick. This's my land and you got no damn right to come in here and — '

'And these two?' Tyrell motioned with the Colt.

On the verge of telling him to go to

hell, Jelnick changed his mind. This time, using his thumb, he indicated the redhead nursing his wrist. 'That there's Johnny DeVane you just winged. Other's Len Tickner.'

'And which of you good, upstanding gents was it that yesterday gunned down the Cross bar A rider?'

DeVane, in the process of wrapping a bandanna around his wrist, looked up, frowning. Tickner's rodent face showed complete confusion.

'What you talking about?' Jelnick asked. 'What rider?'

'Kid named Roy Henkel.'

The man's head canted slightly. 'You riding for them?'

'Might be.'

'Tough about the kid,' Jelnick shrugged. 'But go look someplace else. Ain't none of us had a hand in anything like that.'

'Yeah . . . tough. But not as tough as it's going to be on the one who killed him.' Now it was Tyrell's turn to dredge up a frown. 'Found signs down by an old mining shack. Got the impression the kid was maybe following cattle tracks and stumbled across something that proved detrimental to his health.'

'Mister,' Jelnick breathed, 'consider yourself lucky you're holding that gun! I've had more'n a gutsful of your accusations. You got proof of something against us, you take it to the sheriff. Until then — get the hell off my land!'

'Be my pleasure. As for proof . . . How about a Winchester with some interesting markings?'

'You got nothing!' Jelnick sneered, but both the twisting of his lips and the shaping of his words were slowed by the flickering of realization. 'Now get the hell out of my sight!'

In that moment Tyrell was pretty sure he knew which of the three had killed Henkel. He smiled down at Frank Jelnick.

'Be my pleasure. But while I'm at it, you fellers keep your hands where they'll not be tempted. Ground around here looks kind of hard for grave-digging.'

Johnny DeVane's malevolent gaze stayed fixed upon Tyrell's back until he disappeared from sight.

'That bastard's dead. I'm gonna kill him, Frank! First chance I get, I'm gonna kill him!'

'Didn't do so damned good when you had the chance, did you?' Jelnick sneered, wheeling back to the house.

# 6

Cradlestone at night looked little different from so many other towns through which Tyrell had passed. Possibly a little larger and better laid out than most, but that was all. Near to where he'd entered the broad main street, a church was under construction, its high-pitched roof partially completed, thrusting toward heaven. He rode on, reading storefront signs, looking for the livery stable and hotel.

After turning his back on the 7-Bar, he'd swung east, continuing without haste until finding cattle held under the Bent Arrow iron. From there on he'd travelled with added caution, having no desire to run into the Farradays or any of their crew.

Spring roundup was long over and most ranches would have already completed their drives to chosen shipping points. Cross bar A, according to Denver Crowley, had managed theirs while they still had most of their crew. That being so, if the scattered and recently branded stock he'd encountered were any kind of measure, it meant Broken Arrow still held what had to be one of the largest herds in the valley.

There was water, too, though perhaps not in the same abundance as its neighbor. Crossing the land he'd come upon the shapes of three windmills limned against the night sky.

What seemed a good while later, with daylight all but gone, he picked up the smell of wood smoke and, soon afterward, the dim glow of lamplight. He went in closer, keeping within the shadows of a small grove of trees, maintaining sufficient distance so as not to arouse any dogs that might be in the yard. Farraday's headquarters was rambling and impressive, and with hardly any sounds at all coming from it. He stayed a while, watching, until the smoke floating lazily from the cook-shack chimney reminded him that it had been a long while since breakfast.

From Frain's Livery & Feed Barn, after ensuring the roan would be properly taken care of, he carried his Winchester and war bag, still wrapped in his bedroll, to the better of the town's two hotels.

Next morning he was up and out on the street in time to watch Cradlestone stirring to life, suddenly unsure of what he would do with the rest of the day. Part of his mind told him he ought to be moving on, that there was nothing for him here. Another part echoed Dana Lane's words ... *I believe there's a reason for you riding into our lives.*

Most of his life Webb Tyrell had been forced to live with the harshness of reality, to give scant attention to fantasies, only occasionally permitting himself new dreams. But here he was, on a street in a strange town, with nothing to hold him but words a dark-haired girl had quietly spoken. It made no sense.

He started walking aimlessly. At a store that had only just opened its doors he picked up matches, papers, and a sack of tobacco. At the café where he'd eaten the night before, after discovering the hotel dining-room already closed, he ate breakfast, and thirty minutes later was back on the street, across from the red brick building housing the bank, looking at the three windows on the upper floor. Two were blank; the centre one boasted the painted legend: VANCE J. BERESFORD, ATTORNEY AT LAW.

Returning to the hotel he parked himself in one of the wicker chairs on the veranda, leisurely building a smoke while watching people move along the boardwalks, riders and wagons rolling in and out of town . . . early shadows taking shape.

One of the light vehicles might well be carrying a pine-boxed Roy Henkel back to Cross bar A, for they'd be burying the boy today. He wondered if anyone other than a preacher and those at the ranch would be there . . . And if it mattered.

Again he could see the final grimace on the kid's face, hear his dying words: '*Double-crossing bast* — ' Had the accusation been directed at him? Or had the kid been confused, taken him for someone else? Like the party who'd dropped him . . . ?

The clerk came outside to finish a short cigar he'd only recently lit, a newspaper tucked under his arm. His glance slid to the man who sat with long legs stretched out in front of him. Though dressed in the attire of most rangemen, there was about him a difference. His dark-blue shirt was fresh, the whipcords and canvas brush-jacket, though not new, clean . . . his boots wiped to a light shine. And there was the thonged-down holster, the Colt with its smoothly polished rosewood stocks within easy reach. There were questions the clerk would have asked, but discretion stilled his tongue.

Smiling, he said, 'Early copy, if you'd like to read it,' and offered the newspaper.

Tyrell straightened up, took it from him. 'Obliged.'

'My pleasure,' said the clerk, and went back to his desk, on the way trading the smile for a small frown.

The *Cradlestone Clarion*, an eight-page weekly, bore the current day's date. Most of the stories the paper carried meant little to him; the names featured, even less. Except for a three-inch item at the bottom of the first page that told of the expected arrival of Florence Anderson, widow of Nathanial Anderson who'd died in a riding accident three months earlier. It had, according to the report, been nineteen years since Mrs Anderson departed Cradlestone, and this, her first return visit, was believed to be in some way connected with the Cross bar A ranch, and the rest of her late husband's estate.

Tyrell put aside the paper, began to spin another smoke, wondering who had given the story to the newspaper. Beresford, Dana Lane's lawyer? The friend who was supposed to have contacted the woman . . . ? Or maybe the party operating the small post and telegraph office?

He was lighting the quirly when, coming along the street, a wagon with a hulking character nursing the reins pulled at his attention. As it drew closer, long, stringy black hair could be seen hanging from under the driver's shapeless hat, several days' dark growth on the wide, vacuous face. But it was the man on the yellow horse, on the far side of the vehicle, who interested him more.

Drawing abreast of the hotel, the rider tossed a casual glance at the building. Then, leaning from his saddle, he spoke to the driver, handing him what looked like a folded sheet of paper. The man nodded without bothering to turn his head.

Tyrell went on smoking while Idaho Smith steered the claybank across the street. At the hotel he dismounted, looped reins around the leather-slicked wood of the hitch rack, then came up on to the veranda. Keeping his back to the street, he folded his arms, smiling as he leaned a narrow rump against the railing.

'Kinda surprised to find you out there yesterday, Webb. Been an age.'

'Uh-huh. A long time.' Tyrell flicked the cigarette butt into the street. 'Something on your mind?'

Smith's shoulders made a slight lift and fall. 'Figured it best not to let them know you and me was acquainted. Leastways, not just yet.' Still smiling, he asked, 'You working for the girl?'

'I'm not taking her money, if that's what you're asking.'

'Glad to hear it, Webb. Though it still puzzles me how I come to find you out there.'

Tyrell narrowed his eyes up at the other man.

'There were reasons. Mostly mine.' His glance flicked at Smith's right hip. 'Your gun's been bought by Farraday, huh?'

'Hired, Webb. Hired. Never bought.'

Further down the street Tyrell could see the buckboard halted at the general store, the driver climbing to the ground. He stood up.

'You the reason the girl's crew's so whittled down?'

Idaho's smile widened. 'I take orders, Webb. Take 'em and do the best I can.'

'Farraday must want that spread pretty damned bad.'

'Never asked him about it. Long as the man pays . . . what the hell do I care.' Thin arms unfolded, dropped to his sides. 'So if you're not working for her, what holds you here?'

Tyrell shrugged. 'Like you just said: why should you care?'

'Because we're the same breed, you and me. That's why. We're — '

'No,' Tyrell cut in easily. 'That we're not. I'd like to think I was a lot more particular about what I do and who I do it for.'

The lanky one grew silent, his gaze hardening.

'Ride on, *amigo*.' The flesh under the thin moustache paled when lips pulled taut. 'You're not getting paid to dally . . . and I'd like it better that we never had to tangle.'

'Any chance of it?' Tyrell frowned.

Smith laughed softly, shook his head.

'Hell, man — you were never stupid. Already you've made enemies of the Farradays. What do you think?' A thin sigh whistled through his teeth. 'We've known each other a long while, Webb. Even had ourselves a disagreement or two. But it's never gone further than that.' With the sharpness of a thunderclap, the last trace of humor deserted him. 'Let's keep it that way. Mosey on. For old times' sake.'

'And if I don't?'

'Then stay clear of Cross bar A.'

'Same question, Idaho.'

Smith shrugged, made a gesture that said he'd tried.

'Then it could come to where I might just have to kill you.' Before Tyrell could respond, he hauled himself up straight and stiff. 'I can, Webb. Easy. I was always good, you know that. Now . . . I'm whole heap better.'

# 7

It was still too early in the day, with not enough customers in the Jack O' Diamonds to keep the bartender busy. When Tyrell parked his elbows on the mahogany, the bald, moon-faced apron had a newspaper spread out in front of him, thoughtfully stroking his waxed moustache as he read.

'Beer,' Tyrell told him, when at last he deigned to come over to take his order. When he did, it was to give the tall, expressionless man a careful once-over, checking him against the umpteen faces he had filed in memory. Something made a faint click, though not sharp enough to warrant a question. But while the man worked behind the bar, the feeling that he'd seen Tyrell somewhere, sometime before, gathered strength.

'New in town?' It was both an

observation and a question when he slid the beer across the wood.

Tyrell nodded and, anticipating another question, turned, allowing his gaze to take in the rest of the saloon, finding no recognizable face. By the time he returned to his drink he was thinking again of Dana Lane, of Denver . . . and of the Farradays.

★　★　★

At the run-down house at 7-Bar, Len Tickner's weasel face screwed up pensively, hooded eyes returning to his companion on the other side of the lamplit front room.

'How's the arm?'

Flopped out in a decrepit armchair, Johnny DeVane lifted his crudely bandaged wrist. 'Stiff,' he scowled bitterly.

Tickner nodded, not caring. 'Wonder who the hell Frank's supposed t'be dealin' with — why it's gotta be so damn secret.'

'Wouldn't think about it too loud,' DeVane cautioned, scratching his stubbled chin. 'Jelnick don't look like much, but when he tells you something, you best listen.'

'Oh, I'm doin' that. Only there better be the pay-off he's promised.'

'Yeah,' Johnny agreed. 'Layin' around like we been doin' . . . it's driving me nuts.'

'Bein' broke don't help neither.' Tickner stretched thin legs, sank deeper into the other of the two shabby chairs, studying the redhead. 'Never figured you to be scared of him, Johnny.'

Johnny DeVane rose moodily. 'Watch your mouth, little man. I'm scared'a nobody! Not Jelnick, not nobody!'

'How 'bout the rannie burnt your hand? Reckon you'd face up to him again?'

'Not like this.' Again DeVane displayed his injured wrist. Then he laughed softly, drily. 'But he's already dead, Lennie. Only he don't yet know it.'

Len Tickner pulled his small frame upright, a dull gleam in reptilian eyes. 'How you figure that?'

★  ★  ★

Vance Beresford owned a small house at the far end of town, a property just large enough to provide for his bachelor needs. In the process of pouring himself a drink, he froze at the sound of carefully spaced knocking. Quickly he closed the book of scrawled notes and drawings, putting it away in a drawer of a nearby cabinet before heading to the back of the house.

Opening the door, he swore softly. Standing to one side of the opening, clear of the light, was the bearded Frank Jelnick.

'What the blazes are you doing here?' he rasped, searching the dark, knowing that, unless someone was watching from the grove behind the house, they could not be seen. 'I told you — '

'Had to chance it,' Jelnick muttered,

pushing quickly into the kitchen, waiting until Beresford shut the door before continuing: 'That kid who found us at the shack . . . he's dead.'

'Damnit, wasn't that why you went after him?' Beresford asked with stifled anger. 'Anyway,' he added more calmly, 'the Lane girl was in town soon afterward. She told me.'

'She also tell you about the scudder who took the body back to their spread?'

The bigger man's forehead ridged up. With a nod of his head, he heeled about, heading for the sitting-room where he closed the drapes at the front windows before grudgingly pouring Jelnick a drink.

'What about him?'

'Stranger. Name of Tyrell. Rode out to 7-Bar yesterday. A hard-ass — and real sudden with a gun. Johnny tried to draw on him and got burned for his trouble.' Jelnick wiped the back of a hand roughly across his mouth, pausing to reflect upon something before taking the glass. 'Never came right out and said it, but he's got to be working for the girl.'

'And you risked coming here to tell me that?'

'Also to warn you to stay clear of that shack. This Tyrell, he found it. Figured it's been used as a meeting place, or something, and might be the kid seen whatever it was and it got him killed.'

'It did.' Beresford took a sip of the whiskey which no longer tasted nearly as good as usual. 'That it?'

'No . . . ' Jelnick half-emptied his glass, moved his feet uneasily. 'Boys are getting edgy, cooped up there.'

'Too bad for them.' Beresford's eyes hardened. 'They still know nothing about our arrangement?'

'Nah. Only that I got something going on the side.'

'Then keep it that way. What I've got here is far too big for any slip-ups by a bunch of fools!'

Jelnick's hairy countenance flushed warmly. 'Told you they know nothing.

Besides, I can keep them in line.' He broke off to kill the rest of his drink. 'Thing is, we're short on coin, and no way to raise a dime since you ordered hands off Cross bar A beef.'

'And I meant it. For the next few weeks that ranch has to appear worth top dollar, in every respect.'

'Well then . . . ?' Jelnick looked first into his empty glass, then at the lawyer.

Beresford glared scornfully back at him, this man he'd met when first hanging out his shingle in Black Ridge, Kansas. He'd been hired to defend him against a charge of murder, a case that never got to court, for Jarvis, as Jelnick was then known, managed to break free from the holding cell, leaving behind a dead jailer.

He'd never been recaptured, and Beresford forgot all about him. Until, a few months ago, right here in Cradle-stone, called to defend Johnny DeVane on a drunk and disorderly charge, they met again.

An opportune meeting, for it happened within days of receiving the pathetic letter Flo Anderson had written to old Edward Armstrong, not knowing that he'd died and someone else now owned the practice. The letter had been one more attempt to extract money from Nat Anderson. The moment they'd set eyes upon each other, Beresford realized how he could use Jelnick in putting into action an idea which had been shaping up in his mind.

Readily Jelnick agreed to help, though Beresford remained unsure whether it was because of fear that the lawyer would turn him in if he didn't — or simply the smell of big money.

Until then, Jelnick, Johnny DeVane, and Len Tickner had been running a rag-tag operation, supposedly raising a scraggly herd, but earning a living mostly by rustling Cross bar A and occasionally Bent Arrow beef, selling it to mining slaughterhouses.

So far it had worked out well, to the

point of speeding up events by arranging Nat Anderson's 'accidental' death.

'Well?' Jelnick repeated. 'You going to help out with a few dollars? The boys need to let off some steam. Matter of fact, I could do with some of the same.'

'You forgetting something?' Beresford asked caustically. 'Like the reason we last met at the shack?' He started reaching for the bottle, then quit. 'Because three weeks ago I told you what had to be done, and still that old coot is walking around.'

Jelnick fiddled with his empty glass, remembering when a stone rolling down the slope of the hollow had alerted him to the fact that they were not alone, that someone — that Henkel kid — was watching and listening to him and Beresford. And right at that moment Beresford had been complaining that his orders to get rid of Denver Crowley had still not been executed.

As it turned out, he'd been lucky to ride the kid down, though not so lucky in doing it in front of someone he hadn't even known was down there at the seep. Worse, he had little doubt Tyrell now knew it was him he'd seen . . . he'd found his Winchester. For the briefest moment he considered telling about it, and as quickly changed his mind. Beresford was in bad enough mood. And anyway, if Johnny was given his way, Tyrell would no longer be any problem.

It was uncharacteristic of the man, but right then Frank Jelnick squirmed, avoiding Beresford's large, demanding eyes.

'Hell, I told you — there was no way to get it done like you wanted. I watched their place for days, but if ever the old bugger was off it, it was when I wasn't around.' Meaningfully, he dumped the empty glass on the table upon which stood the open bottle. Beresford ignored the hint. 'I swear, it's like he smelled something — like he was sticking around on purpose.'

Beresford got rid of his own glass, reached under his immaculate gray coat for his wallet, and freed a few small bills.

'Use this to pacify those other two. Just make sure they don't start any trouble when they come to town. As for you ... you've already let too much time pass. I want Denver Crowley put out of the way — and I want it done tonight! By the time that stage rolls in tomorrow, I want to know he's dead!'

# 8

Supper over, the Farradays had moved to the large front room, Morgan Farraday to his usual place as family head, hands folded under his chin, staring into the flickering glow of the fireplace. On his lap lay the current issue of the *Clarion* which Idaho had that afternoon brought back from town, along with the mail and supplies.

Philip, the youngest of the clan, a smaller, trimmer version of his brother, occupied another of the heavy leather-covered chairs. A brooding, quiet-speaking boy who, because of a stupid prank played upon him while still at school, had lost the sight in his right eye. Presently, the good eye was slitted, almost closed, but focused on his father.

Once there had been much evidence of a caring woman's touch in that rambling house, but that was a long time ago, when Morgan Farraday's wife was still alive. Now there was no sign of Helena ever having been near. A handsome but never beautiful woman, she'd succumbed to pneumonia while the boys were still very young; Roley nine, and Phil just seven. It had been left to their father and a Mexican housekeeper to raise them.

So far that evening there'd been little talk. Now Phil asked: 'Something about the Anderson woman's return bothering you?'

His father glanced up sharply. Though two years younger than his brother, Phil had always been the more perceptive.

'Bothering me? No . . . ' He tossed aside the paper. 'Been thinking about it, that's all. Like . . . if somehow she could get someone such as Judge Thackery to — '

'That old soak,' Roley sneered from where he lay full length upon the couch, hands cupped behind his head.

'That old soak,' his father reminded him, 'still has influential friends at the county judiciary. If she can get him on her side, she could well win.'

Philip pushed up out of his chair and moved to the taboret on which a variety of bottles was displayed.

'I still think that after nineteen years she'd need a better reason than simply claiming to be Anderson's widow and rightful heir.'

The oldest of the clan thoughtfully stroked his short, graying beard. 'Maybe she has. Flo Anderson was a number of things, but never stupid.'

A small smile materialized on Roley's face. He'd been only a pup then, and it had been less than a year since his mother had died, but he remembered Aunt Flo. Oh, yeah, he remembered Aunt Flo . . . her visits during the day . . . the noises he'd heard in what had been his parents' bedroom . . . the sights seen through a keyhole . . .

Phil turned, asking if either of the others wanted a drink.

'Yeah,' Roley yawned. 'A good stiff one.' And suddenly he was chuckling.

'Something you find amusing?' his father grunted, getting to his feet.

'Thinking,' Roley grinned. 'Just thinking.'

★　★　★

A while ago full dark had dropped its cloak over Cradlestone, and again Webb Tyrell, at a loose end and restless, found himself in the Jack O' Diamonds. Had there been a game of poker available he might have invited himself in. He considered another beer, caught the barkeep again giving him furtive glances, and decided against it. The man had questions, was trying to muster whatever he needed to ask him.

He built a fresh smoke, got it lighted, and shook his head when the barman hurried over to refill his glass. 'Maybe later,' he said, and aimed himself at the batwings.

There was a chill in the air, perhaps a

signal of an early fall. The town was quiet, but then it was Thursday, and mid-month. He started walking, slowly, and gradually the feeling he'd felt only lightly earlier, now gained strength. Somewhere, something wasn't right . . . He'd had those hunches before, too often to ignore them, that of a shadow trailing him, waiting to pounce.

At the older end of town he halted across the street from another saloon, one from which the strains of a skillfully manipulated Spanish guitar drifted. He listened, and then a woman's soft, clear contralto reached out to him like the song of the Lorelei.

About to cross the street, to answer the lure of the music, he pulled up short. A dark figure, left arm loaded, had pushed through the swing doors, moving to one of the three horses waiting at the rack.

Tyrell drew back into the shadows, watching while Frank Jelnick hurriedly packed four bottles into a saddlebag, lifted himself aboard the steeldust, and took off.

It seemed a hell of a long way to come for a few bottles, but then each man's thirst makes its own demands. For a while he stayed in the cover of the shadows, the feeling of impending danger rising to full height, like a wild mustang ready to smash unshod hoofs into the skull of its would-be captor.

★　★　★

Cross bar A was in total darkness. The dog that once had roamed the yard, who had signalled the approach of man or beast, had grown old, surrendered itself to whatever hereafter was reserved for such as he. Nat Anderson had loved that hound, and because he had, he'd never replaced it. And so there was no one to warn of the shadowy figure that skulked along the outskirts of the yard, six-gun clenched in its fist.

Sound asleep, Denver Crowley was

dreaming of a time of long trail drives, of saloon fights and painted women, when something scratched at his consciousness. He turned over, went back to sleep, and returned to that day when, after every other peeler had failed, he'd brought that ornery buck-skin down to a slow and respectful walk. He smiled in his sleep, and then abruptly his eyes shot open, ears preened toward the sound that had come from the yard.

He lay still, listening. It came again — unidentifiable, like the scrape of a boot, but not so. Something else. A skittering pebble . . . a tumbleweed . . .

Making every effort not to wake the quietly snoring Stretch who'd put in a long and heavy day, Denver rolled back the covers, drew the Smith & Wesson from its holster hanging close to the head of his bunk, and crept to the bunkhouse door.

Carefully he raised the latch, eased the door open, stood dead still, listening. A distant cricket called to any of its kind who would hear; a frog croaked its annoyance, and a soft breeze hissed the world back to silence.

It came again — a quiet skittering noise, close to the bunkhouse.

Denver eased the door open, and the sound reached him again louder. He cursed silently, thumbed back the hammer of the old gun, and pulled the door wide open, recognizing the sound a pebble made when tossed.

For a while there was nothing but silence, a moment the moon chose to peek from behind a thin bank of clouds — the moment the hidden Frank Jelnick, aching for another drink from the fourth bottle in the saddlebag, chose to level the Colt and trigger off two fast shots.

Denver reeled back, gasping. Then, legs which had straddled ponies wild and tame, which had carried him proudly through the streets of Dodge, Abilene, Cheyenne . . . once, even Chicago and San Francisco, failed him. He felt himself going down, heard

Stretch's alarmed shout . . . thought of Dana who, as had Nat, he loved as a daughter . . .

Then darkness, like a giant eraser, wiped away everything.

# 9

Though fully dressed, Dr Sam Halyard looked as if he'd just had his sleep disturbed. Small and wiry, he ran a hand over roughly combed gray hair before opening the door wider to admit his caller.

'Got the note you left at the hotel last night,' Tyrell told him.

'Early this morning would be more accurate,' Halyard quietly grunted, and shut the door. 'Right after getting back from the Anderson ranch.'

Tyrell removed his hat. 'How bad is he, Doc?'

'He's been shot,' Halyard replied, going to an old roll-top desk, dropping into the chair angled in front of it. From there he performed an unhurried inventory of the tall, unsmiling man before beckoning to another chair. 'Fortunately, not too seriously.'

Tyrell waved aside the invitation. 'Not what your note says . . . '

'His idea. Figured if someone wanted him dead it might be worthwhile letting them think they'd virtually succeeded.' The medico chuckled tiredly. 'Which is why I wrote what I did. The clerk was sure as hell to read it, and by now at least half a dozen more know.' Abruptly he ditched the humor. 'But it'll take a lot more than a shoulder wound and a bump on the head to keep that old war horse down. And permanently so is obviously what the dirty, bushwhacking bastard intended. Shot at him twice. Missed the first time. Either figured his second shot did the job, or tucked tail and ran.' He sighed heavily. 'That's it. All I can tell you. Except that the old feller asked that I try and contact you — get you to come out if you were still around.'

Tyrell put his hat back on. 'Thanks, Doc.' Turning to the door, he hesitated. 'How'd you know I'd be at the hotel?'

Wearily, the doctor lifted himself out

of the chair. 'Denver's guess. As for going out there — don't. At least not today. Let him get some rest. Besides,' and now he squinted thoughtfully at the younger man, 'he said you'd probably first want to see something here in town.'

Tyrell's face remained blank. Then he nodded. 'Quite a character, isn't he?'

'And one of the best.' For a long breath there was only silence in the spacious room. 'He was talking about the noonday stage, wasn't he?' Dr Sam Halyard finally asked.

On the way back to the hotel Tyrell slowed when hearing the sound of horsemen approaching from his rear. At first he paid them no attention, but when they were about to move past him, he flicked a glance to the right, recognizing first the dappled white that strutted proudly between the two other horses. His gaze lifted to the stern, spade-bearded face of Morgan Farraday, shifted to the right and found his hefty son, Roley. The third rider was someone he'd not seen before.

Of the three he appeared to be the youngest, sitting very erect in the saddle, looking straight ahead, a stolid expression upon a face that was not unpleasant to look at. A black leather patch covered his right eye.

None of the three seemed to notice him.

\* \* \*

Thanks probably to the newspaper item, that day there were more than the usual to welcome the stage. Among them a young man wearing a marshal's badge, whose eyes moved unobtrusively from one to the other of those gathered at the Wells Fargo depot, always returning to where a short distance away, a man in a dark flat-crowned hat had his back propped against an awning support.

Foremost in the waiting group was a tall, heavily built man in a gray suit who, instinctively, Tyrell took to be the lawyer of whom Dana Lane had spoken. Allowing his gaze to drift, to follow Vance Beresford's, he found Morgan Farraday almost concealed in the shade on the other side of the broad street.

A shout rang loud from far down at the west end of town, then, growing rapidly louder, came the racket of hoofbeats, of wheels grinding up dirt. Within just a short while the Concord, rocking on leather thoroughbraces, pulled up at the depot. The driver set the brakes, threw down the reins to the stocktender, a fat mailbag to the superintendent, then peeled off his gauntlets and climbed down from the box.

First out of the stage was a trim, pink-faced young man in a brown suit of current fashion. Small-mouthed, with a chin that tapered sharply, he could have been a few years on either side of twenty. Ignoring everyone, he turned back to the open door of the coach to help another passenger to the ground.

The face of the woman he assisted was veiled, but, judging from her movements, she was into middle age. Her hair was a rusty red; hat, dress and gloves, solid black. All eyes were upon her and the young man as Beresford stepped quickly forward, removing his hat, extending a large hand.

Tyrell brought the making from his pocket, watching while the lawyer arranged for baggage to be taken over to the same hotel he was using. While he did so, from behind her veil, the woman who had to be Flo Anderson, allowed herself a swift appraisal of those there to witness her return. Arriving at the man carefully fashioning a smoke, her roving glance halted, held for a few seconds, then jerked away. Quickly hooking her hand in the crook of Beresford's arm, she allowed herself to be guided along the boardwalk.

The young man trailed a little behind, a faint, disapproving twist on

his mouth while surveying his surroundings.

The small group began to break up.
One of them, Tyrell noticed, was the
Jack O' Diamond's bartender, a bowler
hat now covering his bald head, smiling
as he started back to his place of
work. Across the street, the shaded
spot Farraday had occupied was now
deserted.

'Your name Tyrell?' a voice asked.

Tyrell turned to look down into the
face of the town marshal.

★    ★    ★

From the other side of Ben Paulson's
desk, Tyrell asked, 'Something about
me being in your town you don't like?'

Avoiding a direct answer, Paulson
said, 'Wanted to talk to you, that's all.
Miss Lane told me about you seeing
Roy Henkel shot, bringing his body
back to the ranch.'

'Then you know everything.'

Paulson brushed uncomfortably at

thick, wavy black hair. 'Everything I've been told,' he corrected.

'Well, then,' Tyrell said slowly, 'supposing I was to tell you I think I know who gunned the kid down?'

'Name a name.'

'Frank Jelnick, runs a — '

'I know who Jelnick is.' Paulson's jaw tightened. 'You got proof?'

'No.'

The marshal let out his breath, made an exasperated, empty-handed gesture. 'Then there's nothing I can do.'

Tyrell studied him, making no effort to hide what he was doing. Ben Paulson neither flinched nor moved his own gaze.

'Find what you were looking for?'

'Nothing personal,' Tyrell answered, getting up from the hardback chair, waiting as the marshal also rose. 'I understand the limits of your authority. As I'm sure does Miss Lane.'

Suddenly Paulson's smooth face was several shades darker.

'What's that supposed to mean?'

Tyrell gave a slight shrug of dismissal.

'No more than what I said.' But in that instant he had more than just a good idea that the shorter man's feelings for Dana Lane went somewhat deeper than he'd so far allowed his words to indicate.

'You — planning to go back to the ranch?' The question was spoken with apparent difficulty.

Tyrell hesitated. If the hotel clerk had read Halyard's note, if the story of Denver's shooting had started the rounds, it evidently hadn't reached the marshal's ears. For the time being he chose to leave it that way.

'There's that possibility,' he said.

'Get something straight, Tyrell,' Ben Paulson warned, and if before he'd made an effort to keep his feelings under wraps, he made none now. 'Miss Lane has enough problems. I don't want her hurt, I don't want any more trouble brought her way!'

'Last thing intended. I'd — '

'Your kind always bring trouble,' Paulson cut in sharply.

A cloud moved behind Webb Tyrell's eyes, but when he spoke again his voice was almost gentle.

'What is my kind, Marshal?'

Paulson realized he'd used a poor choice of words, the kind that invited requital. But he said, 'A goddamned gunhawk.'

A little sadly, Tyrell looked down at him, and without a word left the office.

\* \* \*

By late afternoon there were many more in the Jack O'Diamonds than had been there at that time any previous day of that week. Behind the long bar the bald apron with the waxed moustache was back on duty. Shoving a beer in front of Tyrell, his head lifted, eyes widening apprehensively.

A hand fell heavily upon Tyrell's shoulder.

'You and me, bucko,' a voice announced harshly, 'we got unfinished business to settle.'

# 10

Tyrell made a slow half-turn of his head. 'Get your hand off me.'

Roley Farraday's grip fastened painfully. 'I said we got unfinished business!'

Coming sharply around, Tyrell knocked aside his hold. 'And I said to keep your paws to yourself.'

At a table against the wall, Idaho Smith, who'd arrived in town a while after his employers, spoke softly to the youngest of the Farradays.

'Be an idea to stop whatever your hothead brother's tryin' to start. Else he could just be inviting himself an early burial. That's no ornament, that Colt that feller's wearing.'

Still facing the heaviest of the Farradays, Tyrell said, 'Now go away. I don't want to fight you,' and turned back to his untouched drink.

'Like I thought! Yeller!'

Phil came up next to his brother. 'Roley, let it go.'

'The hell I will. No lousy drifter's going to make me look stupid in front of Pa! 'Specially not when he's got to use a boot to do it — and when I wasn't looking!'

The barman pressed anxiously against the counter.

'Gents, please! You got a problem — take it outside.'

'Shut up!' Farraday snarled. 'This don't concern you!'

Watching the reflection of the two behind him in the backbar mirror, Tyrell said, 'I'll tell you for the last time. I don't want to fight you.'

'What you want and what you're gonna get . . . '

Phil started to speak again, but before he'd managed the second word Roley was grabbing for Tyrell.

Instead of resisting, Tyrell came around easily, shoving forward his left to keep his opponent at a preferred distance while the heel of his wide-open right rammed upward, smashing into the underside of Farraday's nose.

Uttering a strangled howl of pain, wiping at blood pouring from his nostrils, Roley backed off several paces.

Phil pulled himself to his full height.

'Why, you dirty — ' His left shoulder dropped and a tightly-balled fist went rocketing at Tyrell's head. Almost as if moving at his own designated time, Tyrell shifted from its path and sent a right of his own hurtling forward. It caught Phil on the point of his chin, slamming his teeth together, sending him stumbling backward. For a moment he stood, staring glassy-eyed before his knees turned to water.

Face white, blood-smeared and distorted in fury, Roley lunged for the bar, grabbing a bottle that was still half full. He started to swing, but a shot racketing through the saloon froze his hand in mid-air.

Gun pointed businesslike, Ben Paulson strode up to the bar.

'Put it down, Roley. This's as far as it goes.'

'The hell with you! We've only just got started.'

'I said that's it!' the marshal snapped loudly.

Roley Farraday wasted a moment considering the threat. Then, slowly he put the bottle back on the bar, wiped at his nose.

'You made a mistake, Paulson. A mighty big mistake.'

'I've made them before,' Paulson quietly grunted. 'Now, collect your brother and get on home.' He nodded to where Idaho Smith was standing. 'Take him with you.' Eyes hardening, his gun nosed toward Tyrell. 'Same goes for you. Clear out!'

\* \* \*

A short while earlier, Morgan Farraday had come into Vance Beresford's office, taking a seat without waiting to be invited.

'Well?' he demanded. 'What'd Thackery have to say?'

Though in no reflection of his present mood, the lawyer smiled congenially. When taking the Andersons to the hotel he'd heard about Crowley being shot down, but so far there'd been no word from Jelnick to confirm it.

'About what?'

Farraday leaned forward, beard jutting. 'Don't mess with me, damnit! You know what I'm talking about!'

'Of course . . . though I'm not sure that it's any of your business.' Beresford raised a big, mollifying hand. 'But, since it'll be common knowledge one of these days, I guess there's no harm telling you.' Before continuing, he steepled thick fingers under his chin. 'Turns out the judge can find no reason to regard the documents she presented as anything but authentic.'

'Then . . . that kid is Anderson's?'

'His name is Lionel,' Beresford supplied. 'Named after her father, she says. And she has a birth certificate testifying to the fact that he was born eight months after leaving Cradlestone ... papers to prove she was Nat Anderson's legal wife at the time.'

'Then,' Farraday queried, brow folding into deep corrugations, 'why the hell's she kept it quiet so long?'

Shrugging, Beresford dismantled the steeple.

'Says she didn't. Claims Anderson was privately a mean, tight-fisted son-of-a-bitch, who beat her, threw her out with barely a penny to her name. After leaving here she travelled as far as what money she had would take her, eventually working her way to San Francisco — where the child was born. Says she wrote to Anderson, begging help, but he never answered any of her letters.'

'Could have a time proving it.'

'There's some evidence that she did. Among old Armstrong's papers are letters telling him the same thing, begging him to approach Anderson on her behalf.' Beresford shrugged again. 'After that she claims to have given up . . . took whatever work she could get, slaving to raise, feed and educate a sick child.'

'You know I want Cross bar A range,' the rancher said, thoughtfully fondling his short beard. 'And you've already got my written offer to present to Flo, if and when her claim succeeds. 'But,' questioning eyes lifted to the heavy man on the other side of the desk, 'there's something I don't savvy. If you're representing the Lane girl . . . '

'Correction. I have not been retained by Miss Dana Lane; nor do I represent her. I have tried to assist, advise her, and nothing more. The same applies to Mrs Anderson — in case you were alluding to a possible conflict of interests.'

'All right,' Farraday grunted impatiently. 'Explain.'

'It's quite simple. Nat Anderson appointed Edward Armstrong — *his future partners, or successor* — to be the executor of his estate. Which is all that I am. As such it is my duty to first ensure that all claims against the estate are legally settled. Which is precisely what I'm doing.'

Farraday allowed that to sink in before asking: 'And now you think Thackery will rule in the widow's favor?'

'Or her son's.' It was the lawyer's turn to frown. 'However, in order to protect himself, he might insist that the issue be tested in court — perhaps at county-seat level.'

'Thing is,' Farraday wanted to know, 'can you trust him?'

Beresford laughed. 'Leave the honorable judge to me.'

'Still,' Farraday snorted, showing his displeasure when he got up, 'that sort of thing could take months.'

'And cost a great deal of money.'

'Go on.'

Beresford quit his own chair. 'Think about it.'

Farraday did, and when he turned

away, he was smiling.

He was at the door when Beresford said:

'You knew her when she lived here, didn't you, Morgan? Flo Anderson . . . '

Farraday lost his smile. 'What if I did?'

'I imagine she must have been quite a looker in those days.'

'She was.' Farraday nodded, remembering.

'You and her — you get along all right?'

*　*　*

Morgan Farraday shoved into the saloon right after the marshal had issued his orders to Tyrell, Idaho Smith, and Farraday's sons to clear out. He stood for a moment, glaring at Paulson, the gun held on his eldest boy, and the bloody handkerchief Roley had pressed to his nose.

'What the hell's going on here?' he demanded, strutting purposefully forward, all but shouldering the marshal aside.

'Your boys can tell you on the way home.'

'Damnit!' Farraday fumed. 'I asked you!'

'Very well.' Ben Paulson holstered his gun. 'Way I understand it, Roley forced a fight on Tyrell here — which didn't work out too well for him. Or Phil.'

Turning to his boys, their father jerked his head at the door. They moved without a word. But not before the youngest paused to stare balefully at the man who had knocked him off his feet. When they were out of the saloon, Farraday swung toward Tyrell.

'This is the second time you've pulled a stunt like this.'

'Hold on, Mr Farraday, I told you it was Roley who — '

'I'm talking to him, damnit!' Farraday rasped, dismissing Paulson. 'There'll be no third time,' he went on, glaring up at Tyrell. 'If there is, you'll regret the day you were born!'

'I'll keep it in mind,' said Tyrell.

'And a good time for doing it would be while heading hell and gone out of this country!'

# 11

Distaste smearing his narrow face, the young man who'd arrived on the stage with Flo Anderson allowed his gaze another slow tour of the hotel dining-room.

'If this is the best this jerkwater town's got,' he muttered, 'it's going to be a hell of a long stay.'

'You hush your mouth and mind your manners,' Flo told him, a mounting irritation evident in her tone.

Lionel leaned back indolently, smiling at her. In her mid-forties, even with hennaed hair, a thick layer of powder and rouge, and a figure turned heavy, she was still a reasonably attractive, if brittle-faced women.

'I could use a drink,' he said.

Flo had only been half listening to his complaints, for a moment earlier she'd noticed the man at the table in the far corner of the room — the same one who'd startled her at the stage depot.

'Matter of fact,' the boy went on, 'I could use several.'

Flo would never be sure if it was the mention of drinks that had an image of a Wichita saloon suddenly leaping forth from memory, bringing with it the acrid stench of gunsmoke. Again she tossed a hasty glance at the corner table.

'Know him?' Lionel smiled curiously.

She pretended not to hear.

The boy, all freshened up, but in the same brown suit, stretched politely. 'You hear what I said about a drink?'

'I heard.' Flo's lips thinned angrily. 'And you can forget it. While we're here you'll keep away from saloons. You can also keep your eyes off that waitress!'

Lionel propped his elbows on the table, thrusting his pointed chin at her.

'Listen, if you think I'm sitting around this dump every night, twiddling my thumbs, you're very much mistaken!'

'Keep your voice down!' she hissed.

'And get something good and straight. You'll do as you're told — and like it!'

Small mouth twisting, he rested back again, but before he could frame a retort, Vance Beresford pulled out a free chair, smiling as he seated himself between them.

'We're not going to have any trouble with you, are we, son? Because if we are, I'd be — severely disappointed.' He tossed a quick, meaningful look at Flo before bringing his eyes back to the boy. 'For the next few days you're going to be on your very best behavior. You're going to be an adoring and dutiful son, doing exactly as your mother tells you. Are we very clear on that?'

'Tell him,' Flo said softly but harshly. 'Already the little bastard's starting to act up.' She took a deep breath and, still holding her voice down, said, 'Try not to make it obvious, but get a gander at the feller sitting alone in the back corner — over to your left. Tell me if you know him.'

Beresford picked up the folded

napkin from next to his place setting — and then let it slip from his fingers. Straightening up, after seeming to have some trouble hitching back his chair in order to retrieve it, he shook his head.

'I think I've seen him before. In fact,' she went on even more softly, 'the more I think about it, the more certain I become.'

'And he — bothers you?'

Her head bobbed slowly. 'Don't recollect his name, but he's some kind of damned gunslinger I remember from back in Wichita. Saw him kill some fool in a saloon — an idiot who knew who he was, but just had to try and prove himself better. The law asked him to leave town, even though — and I was there to see everything — it was a clean fight, something he'd tried to avoid.' She waited a moment, remembering more. 'Uh-huh . . . more I think about it, more certain I become.'

Beresford was no longer smiling. 'Think he'll remember you?'

Flo made no reply, for at that

moment Webb Tyrell got up from his table, preparing to leave. She averted her face when he passed by, not lifting it until he was out of the room.

Beresford was frowning heavily. 'Damnit . . . he never even glanced this way. Yet you're worried. Why?'

'I — I don't know. But I'll tell you this. That's one dangerous man who just walked out of here. I don't know him — never spoke so much as a single word to him — but something warns me he could spell trouble if ever we let him get too near us.'

'Now I really could use a drink!' Lionel smirked, eyeing Flo narrowly. 'Methinks perhaps the lady has not told us all.'

If Beresford heard he gave no indication of it. Never a man to put stock in omens, at that moment, looking at the doors through which Tyrell had passed, he had the uneasy feeling that he'd just been presented with one.

The temperature dropped sharply that night, and while most in Cradlestone slept, a rider arrived at Frain's Livery & Feed Barn, a man long, lean and hollow-cheeked, who looked as if he might already have seen sixty hard years go dragging by.

From the livery he tramped wearily to the bigger of the two hotels and rang the bell to rouse the night clerk. Turning the register around, he automatically reached for the pen and scrawled in his name. E. Cradock.

Tired eyes travelled up the short column of names of those already registered. For the longest moment he stood unmoving, then carefully scratched out his entry. Only when it was completely obliterated was the pen returned to its holder.

'Changed my mind,' he said in a dry, whispery voice, like someone with a respiratory disease.

Adding no more, he picked up his

gear. Suddenly fully alert, all thought of sleep banished, he strode to the street door, leaving behind a clerk staring in open-mouthed confusion. On the boardwalk he tried to remember where the hostler had told him the other hotel, the fleabag, was situated.

\* \* \*

Early the following morning Tyrell was in the saddle, the roan, well rested, happy to be out of the stable. He gave the animal its head, letting it choose its own pace as it lit out of Cradlestone.

Anxious to get to Cross bar A, he paid little attention to the tall, haggard-faced figure who'd stopped to watch him from the still-shadowed side of the street.

The moment Tyrell was at town limits, Eli Cradock left the sidewalk, hurrying in the direction of the livery barn, intentions of an early breakfast abandoned. Half-way across the street, he stopped, slowly shaking his head, smiling inwardly. There was no hurry. He'd waited over six years, ridden hundreds of miles to find Webb Tyrell. He could wait a while longer.

Removing his hat, he ran roughened fingers through hair the color of old ash, returning to the sidewalk only when no longer able to see anything of the departing horseman.

But, an hour later, with nothing to make demands upon his time, he was pointed back in the direction of Bill Frain's stable.

* * *

The roan fell into a contented, easy-going lope and, as if it were a signal for a mood change, Tyrell suddenly felt his enthusiasm to be at the Anderson ranch replaced by the feeling of again having a shadow crowding his back.

The wagon road they followed started a slow descent between lifting bulges of rocky outcrops and heavy brush. Ahead, like a newly minted coin, the sun was still slowly lifting itself from behind the hills.

Vaguely, he remembered a song he'd heard describing such a scene, but few words came to mind. Instead his memory shifted abruptly to a woman seated at a small organ, a man at her side and, somewhere there in those murky corridors of time, the strains of another song, a religious song, and a sense of great comfort and joy. Then, just as abruptly, nothing but an emptiness, a vacuum he had so frequently searched.

# 12

Dana was standing on the gallery when Tyrell rode up to the house, hands upon the rail, as if waiting for someone. He had an idea she'd been out there a while, long before hearing his approach.

'Good morning.'

Quietly she returned the greeting. She was dressed much the same as when last he'd seen her, but this time the shirt had a tiny mauve check, and the riding-skirt was of a light gray. She looked tired, dispirited, her face a little drawn.

'Seem kind of down,' he said, leaving the saddle. 'Because of what happened to Denver?'

She came over to the steps, then down to the lowest, where she'd be at his level. 'It's certainly helped.' She tried to smile, but it was a futile effort. 'I wanted him to move into Uncle Nat's

116

room, where he'd be more comfortable, but he'd have none of it. He's in the bunkhouse if you want to see him.'

'Thanks,' he said, but did not move.

He was still having trouble taking his eyes away from her when suddenly she was looking past him, a small smile, a real smile, curving her lips.

'He must have heard you arrive.'

Turning, he found Denver leaning in the bunkhouse doorway. At the cook-shack door stood the *cocinero*, a rifle in readiness. Tyrell stepped back, preparing to walk the roan across the yard.

'I'll see you before I leave.'

A question started on the girl's lips, but all she said was, 'Yes . . . please do that.'

Stretch Norton materialized from somewhere between the buildings, raising a hand in greeting as he approached. Additional to the holstered gun, he carried a Winchester repeater, the stock of which had his initials neatly burnt into it. Taking the reins from Tyrell, he waved him on to where the old ramrod waited.

Gingerly, Denver parked himself on one of the bunks, leaving his visitor to sit wherever he pleased. His left arm was cradled in a heavy sling, and though he tried to conceal it, behind the whiskers a paled face reflected his pain.

Tyrell told him about the note from Dr Sam Halyard.

'Walked right into it,' Denver muttered disgustedly and explained what happened. 'Little more to the right an' he'd've punched my ticket good. But I got lucky. He jes' winged me — knocked me off my pins, bouncin' my head a li'l too hard against one of them bunks. Told the doc to put out that story so's to give me a little time to mend. Ever they come back for a second try, me an' Stretch'll be ready, an' a whole dang lot more careful.'

'Any ideas about it?'

'Plenty, but none that'll hold water.' Tenderly he rubbed the injured shoulder. 'Danged thing itches somethin' fierce,' he grunted, and swiftly changed the subject. 'That woman show up?'

'Uh-huh.'

'Need to ask you a favor. Want you to watch out for Miz Dana while I'm laid up. Stretch's doin' all he can, but . . . ' Letting the rest ride, he leaned forward, like someone about to share a confidence. 'Take my word, the last thing in the world Nat would've wanted was for that — that woman to get her claws on anything connected with this place.'

'Don't have much regard for her, do you?' Tyrell frowned, not liking the ground on which he was starting to tread, but reading in the old man's face something that demanded he listen.

'None a-tall!' The back of his hand wiped harshly across his mouth. 'Ain't fittin' talk twixt men, but jes' so's to protect Miz Dana's interests, there's a need that certain things be said.' The gnarled hand made an even rougher pass at his mouth. 'Thing Nat wanted most was a son he could raise to take over after he passed on. 'Course, when

Miz Dana came along, she more'n filled that need. But let me ask you this. A man feelin' as did Nat . . . you see him kickin' out a wife that was gonna bear him a child?'

'I never knew him,' Tyrell countered.

'I did, and it was the last thing he'd ever've done, regardless of what she was!'

Tyrell stood up. 'Sure you want me to hear this?'

'Sorry,' the oldster mumbled, 'but the worms've been turned loose, so's I might's well let 'em crawl.' He got off the bunk. 'She was a chippy — a goldarned tramp,' he said tightly, making sure his words would not travel beyond the walls of the room, 'an' I think Nat come quickly to realizin' it. But he did nothin', jes' kinda turned inside hisself — went deliberately blind to some of the goings-on around here. 'Specially when he was away. Even to all the spendin' she did on clothes, he said nothin' — like he knew marryin' her'd been a mistake but was too ashamed to admit it. Might've stayed that way, 'cept she went too far, what with them buggy rides over to . . . ' He broke off, possibly deciding he was about to overstep the mark, and once again changed tracks. 'Seen the kid?'

'Uh-huh.'

'What's he look like?'

'Like someone,' Tyrell shrugged after some deliberation, 'who's rubbed up hard against big cities.'

Denver almost spat, remembering in time he was not outdoors. 'About that favor . . . '

'Don't know how much use I'd be to anyone,' Tyrell told him. 'This's the stuff for lawyers and courts to sort out.'

'Would seem so,' Denver agreed. 'But somethin' in my water tells me that ain't where the real sortin' will be done. All I'm askin' is that you stick around a while. I got some money set aside . . . ' In time he saw the slight clouding of Tyrell's face.

Before either could say more there was the scrape of boots and Stretch pushed at the half-open door. 'Rider coming,' he announced, and disappeared.

Denver turned quickly to the bunk, and when moving to the door had his old Smith & Wesson in his good hand.

The rider was still a way off, approaching with no evident haste. They waited, keeping vigil from inside the bunkhouse, until finally Denver muttered:

'It's OK. It's only that danged shyster.'

Tyrell, who had already made that observation, watched Vance Beresford ride up to the house and dismount.

Shoving the pistol down behind his belt, Denver stepped out on to the hard-packed ground.

Beresford was already on the first of the wide steps when Dana came to the door. He removed his hat, saying something not loud enough to carry across the yard. About to mount the next step, he stopped, like someone feeling an unexpected tap on his shoulder. Slowly he turned his head toward the bunkhouse, and for a long moment he stared. Tyrell wondered whose presence it was that caused the sobering of his expression. His or Denver's.

★ ★ ★

A while later, after the lawyer made his departure, Denver, beginning to show signs of fatigue, led Tyrell over to where Dana remained paused at the bottom of the steps. One look at her was all it took to know something was wrong.

'More bad news?' he asked gruffly.

She tried to speak, but could manage no more than a mute nod before tears welled up in her eyes.

'Hey, there — !' he croaked, stepping forward in an effort to console her.

'It's all right,' she told him, producing a handkerchief from a pocket of her skirt, touching it to her eyes.

They waited until she was ready, Denver listening in forced silence and rapidly mounting anger while she talked; Tyrell unable to remember when last he'd felt so completely helpless.

'And that's it,' she finished. 'According to Mr Beresford, Judge Thackery is perfectly willing to accept the documents she presented as valid, though he'd prefer to have everything settled in court at the county capital. But' — she dabbed at another straying tear — 'it seems almost certain that her son, Lionel — '

Denver snorted contemptuously.

' — will be recognized as Uncle Nat's rightful heir.' She took a deep breath. 'Oh, I could contest such a decision . . . but Mr Beresford says it might take months before any finality is reached. And cost a great deal of money — which I do not have.'

'None of my business,' Tyrell put in, noticing that Stretch, still carrying the carbine, was now standing a short distance away. 'But this Beresford feller . . . he offer any suggestions?'

She nodded. 'He knows the condition

we're presently in, knows I can't raise any money to pay for what could be a long drawn-out legal battle.'

'So?' Denver ground out the question. 'What's he sayin'? To forget what Nat wanted — hand over everything to that — that woman and her whelp?'

'In return for a cash settlement,' she answered, avoiding his angry eyes.

'Yeah? Jes' how big a settlement?'

'It — it would have to be worked out. B-but with a court sure to rule in her favor, I — I couldn't expect very much.'

'Wa-ell . . . money or no money, we'll jes' see 'bout that!' Denver's right fist raised to shoulder level in a sign of defiance and threat. 'We'll see what the hell a court has to say after I'm through tellin' a few of the things I know!' His mouth clipped shut, his gaze swinging sharply to Tyrell. 'I'll be double-dee-damned!' he whispered hoarsely.

He had no need to say more, for at that moment, Tyrell knew he'd hit upon another possible reason for someone wanting his mouth permanently shut.

# 13

It was a hard admission for Denver to make, but reluctantly he agreed that a bit more rest might not be the worst idea in the world. Tyrell left him on his bunk and went back out into the sunlight. Stretch was waiting for him, the roan ready to make the return trip. Together they started towards the main house, but after only a few steps, Tyrell pulled up.

'Want to tell me how Anderson died?' he asked. 'Paper I read said his death was accidental.'

'Yeah, accidental,' Stretch drawled. 'Got thrown from his horse — so hard his skull was stoved in. According to coroner's verdict,' he added sardonically.

Tyrell hitched an eyebrow.

'Yeah . . . exactly.' Stretch nodded. 'After finding him, me and Denver did some checking. Found a place where a rope could've been strung between two trees. Found marks rubbed into the bark. Had it been like Denver opined, Nat would've had to be going at a lick to get yanked from leather and bust up like he was.'

'Maybe he was.'

'Also what we reckoned — 'specially if he had someone shooting at him.' He hesitated, glancing back at the house where Dana was still standing. 'Thing is, place we found his body had plenty of rocks, but it was way off from those trees I mentioned.'

'Moved?'

'Know it was. Nat Anderson was no greenhorn. No horse'd toss him that hard. Specially not one he'd been riding for the past five years.' Once more he flung an uneasy glance at the house. 'As for the head injuries . . . Those could've got given him *after* he was already down. Like with a good-size rock.'

'But — no proof?'

'Right. And without any,' Stretch's

mouth set bitterly, 'that baby-faced star-packer wouldn't lift a damn finger.'

★   ★   ★

'Will you for Pete's sake stop complaining!' Flo all but yelled at the young man who paced restlessly. 'Maybe it's not the Ritz,' she allowed, gaze sweeping the front room of the small house into which they had that morning moved, 'but it's more private than the hotel. Which's why Beresford brought us here.'

'It's a dump,' the boy sneered, picking up the brown suit coat from where he'd tossed it over a chair, shrugging into it.

Flo glared at him. 'Where do you think you're going?'

'Out. It's Saturday, and I'm certainly not about to spend what's left of it hanging around here.'

Hands upon well-padded hips, she continued to glare. 'You've never been in a town like this before, sonny boy.

The men out there are mostly a pretty damned hard bunch.'

'Not to worry. I can take care of myself.' From an inside coat pocket he produced a five-shot .32 pistol; one of Colt's New Line models. 'I have this, remember?'

'Lionel, you start drinking and — '

'Not exactly what I had in mind.' He grinned back lewdly.

A while after he'd left she was still standing there, afraid the boy might land himself in some sort of situation, angry that she herself had to be presently confined to this drab, box-like house. A little fun, even a stroll through the town, would be welcome.

Disposing of the thought, she turned toward the kitchen. At a small oval mirror set in a wall coat-rack, she paused to push a few strands of hair back into place, moving her head from side to side for a better inspection of her face.

She was still primping when knuckles rapped politely against the front door.

Expecting it to be the lawyer, for she could imagine no other caller, she went to open it.

A chunky, ruddy-complexioned man in his mid-fifties stood on the narrow porch.

'Yes . . . ?' she queried.

He lifted his hat, exposing tight gray hair.

'Hello, Flo.'

'My God!' Her hand flew to her mouth! 'Morgan! I — I didn't recognize you with that — that beard.'

And, thought Farraday, had I not seen you get off the stage, I'd never have believed you to be the same slim-waisted, blonde creature I once knew so well. 'May I come in?' he asked.

She let him in, closed the door, and invited him to sit.

'Thanks, but I've an appointment within a few minutes. Just stopped by to say hello.' He looked around the room already invaded by early afternoon shadows. 'Your . . . boy around?'

Under the thick layer of powder he saw her features go taut.

'No. He — he stepped out for some air.'

Farraday's eyes made another cursory examination, liking little of what now stood before him: the increased inches, ponderous breasts, the god-awful hair. He said, 'Kind of threw me, hearing you were coming back . . . with a kid.'

A couple more lines harshly gouged the flesh around her mouth.

'Why should that surprise you? Didn't you think I was — ' She bit off the rest, canted her head to the left, eyes narrowing sharply. Then, quite suddenly she was laughing. 'You — you think he might be . . . ?' The laughter turned slightly raucous, ending immediately his expression started to darken. 'No,' she said, shaking her head. 'No, Morgan, he sure as hell isn't yours!'

'Having seen him, I couldn't imagine it,' he returned coldly. 'Doesn't look much like Anderson either.'

'Why, you filthy — !' In one swift move she closed the distance between them, right hand open and sweeping. Farraday caught her wrist, twisted it backward until she winced.

'Don't ever raise your hand to me, woman!' he warned, shoving her away.

'Damn you,' she seethed, massaging her reddened wrist. 'If your mother had to sweat and scrimp to raise you, if you were born sickly and had to live on medication until you were . . . ' Again she chose not to finish, releasing her wrist to wipe at her eyes.

'I'm sorry,' Farraday mumbled. 'I had no right to say that.'

'No. None at all!' She glared at him, face rigid. 'That all you came for? To try and find out if he was maybe yours?'

He shook his head, selecting his words. 'No — mainly to talk about Cross bar A.'

'Then talk.'

'Appears there's a good chance you'll soon own it.'

'Me *or* my son,' she corrected

pointedly. 'What about it?'

He frowned at her. 'Surely Beresford's told you I've made an offer for it — if and when your claim succeeds?'

'So?' Her eyes slitted shrewdly.

'I'm expanding, bringing in more stock. I need extra range.'

'Oh, yes. I heard you'd become a big number while I've been gone.' She smiled coldly. 'All right, Morgan. I know you want it. But any dealings you've got will have to go through Beresford. He'll be handling everything.'

Farraday studied her, remembering the day Nat Anderson had learned of her visits to Bent Arrow, the day he'd come storming up to the house, bursting in before they'd had time to pull on their clothes. He'd been lucky, damned lucky. Had Anderson gunned him down in his bed, not a court in the land would likely have convicted him. Instead, Anderson had calmly and coldly told his wife to get on home, to pack and get out. Then he'd turned his back on the friend who'd betrayed him, and walked out.

From the bedroom window, his body bathed in cold sweat, humiliation and frustration causing him — *him, Morgan Farraday!* — to weep, he'd watched Flo drive the buggy back home. Watched her husband riding to the side of it.

For only one thing had he been grateful. The boys were at school where they'd not been able to witness anything.

'Thanks,' he muttered. 'I thought maybe you'd — '

'Want to stick it to you?' she finished for him, resuming the taunting laughter, only much quieter this time. 'No, Morgan, I've not forgotten how you turned me away when I came to you after Nat kicked me out. But I won't let it interfere with business.' The smile she turned on him dripped acid. 'If yours is the best offer — why then, you'll be the new owner of Cross bar A.'

'What's that mean?'

'Exactly what it sounded like,' she

told him. 'So, if there's nothing else you wish to discuss — good day to you.'

★   ★   ★

Tyrell knew he was taking a risk riding across Bent Arrow range, but there was something he wanted to see again, this time in daylight. When sighting the first windmill, he drew rein. Beyond it was another, on slightly higher ground. And still further away, a third. He sat, trying to make sense of the vague notion that had forced this return ride. The steel structures appeared to be almost in line with each other, albeit a somewhat meandering line . . .

Slowly, based on the few things Denver had told him . . . something he'd personally experienced, an idea was starting to take vague form.

So centred on his thoughts was he that only when the roan softly nickered and pawed the ground did he become conscious of the sound of approaching riders. He looked around, measuring his chances, realizing they were already too close, the terrain too open, to try and make a run for it.

He waited, and within minutes they were hauled up on either side of him, guns drawn. Idaho Smith and a rider who, when he smiled, showed long teeth and too much gum.

Smith was also smiling. Expansively.

'Well, now, what've we got here? What you reckon we got here, Mike? One of them sneaking cow thieves that've been giving us so much trouble?'

# 14

By night Farraday's headquarters had appeared rambling and impressive. It looked so still, except that in late-afternoon sunlight an ephemeral quality hung over everything, the construction of the buildings suggesting an emphasis on haste and the need of the moment.

Idaho Smith and his companion steered directly for the main house, Tyrell, relieved of his gun, riding between them. The place was quiet, with no sign of activity, reminding him it was Saturday, that most of the crew would probably be in town by now. Especially if Bent Arrow paid wages every two weeks rather than once a month.

Hardly had Idaho called to the house when Roley and Philip showed themselves, dressed as if they too were preparing for a night out.

'Got something for you,' Idaho announced. 'Found him snooping on the west range. Figured you boys might enjoy a word with him.' He swung out of leather, gun levelled at his captive, brusquely ordering him to dismount.

Tyrell's boots had barely touched the ground when the one called Mike was at his back, gun prodding.

By the time they were clear of the horses the Farradays were off the veranda. Grinning broadly, Roley shoved forward and without breaking stride let loose a vicious roundhouse. So unexpected was the blow, Tyrell barely had opportunity to move his head. Knuckles crunched into his temple, spinning him around, sprawling him on to the ground. Roley stepped in closer, swinging a boot, crashing it brutally into his side.

'Son of a bitch! I been waiting for that!'

Phil grabbed his brother's arm as he made ready to deliver another kick.

'Don't waste your energy. I've got a

better idea.' He turned to Smith. 'Get him over to the bunkhouse.'

Head spinning, Tyrell felt his arms gripped and, with no attempt made to get him to his feet, found himself being dragged across the yard.

Inside the bunkhouse Hump Sinden, a man of oversize proportions, nose flattened, face scarred from ancient brawls, lay staring contentedly at the ceiling. He liked it when the rest of the crew were away. It was peaceful then for he had the place to himself. It gave him time to dream the dreams he shared with no one, for fear of having them laugh. One day, though, he was . . .

A strident voice shattered his reverie.

'Hump! You hear me? Get your butt out here, *pronto*!'

Tyrell was lifting himself back to his feet when, through eyes still clouded, he saw a mountain of a man hulk into view.

'Want somethin', Phil?' Apprehension echoed in his voice, showed itself in his bearing.

Tyrell recognized him as the driver of the buckboard he'd seen Idaho Smith accompany to town. Long, stringy hair hung in disarray around his head, and he'd still got no closer to a razor.

'See this jasper?' Phil jabbed a thumb at Tyrell. 'I want you to take him apart, piece by piece — I want you to knock the living crap out of him. You understand me?'

The man turned troubled and confused eyes upon Tyrell, slowly shaking his head when bringing them back to Farraday. Lips moved, but before he could utter a word Farraday's gun was out of its holster.

'You hear what I said? I want — '

'Aw, Phil . . . I don't wanna hurt nobody. I don't even know the feller. Why you want I should hurt him?'

'Because I said so, stupid.' Phil pointed the Colt at the big man's groin, scaring him into quick backward movement. 'Now you listen carefully. Do like I tell you, else I'll take them off — one at a time. You know what I'm telling you?'

'Aw, hell, Phil, you shouldn't oughta keep sayin' . . . '

The gun barrel dipped. Lead kicked up dirt between Hump's boots, driving him back still further. 'No, Phil — don't!'

'Then do like you're told, damnit!'

'Do it!' Roley yelled, his own gun fisted.

Tyrell shrugged resignedly. 'It's OK big feller. Do like you're told.' Closing in, he flung a fist at Hump's middle. It was like hitting a tree trunk.

Reacting on pure instinct, Hump's own fist cannonballed, skimming off the side of Tyrell's jaw, but with such power he was sent flying backward, crashing down hard on to his back.

Phil strode quickly to where he'd fallen, getting in his two bits, kicking hard at his left thigh.

'Get up, you bastard. This's where you find out what it means to knock me down in public!'

Tyrell rolled over painfully, resting on an elbow to look up at the tense face. The leather eye-patch gleamed darkly while teeth showed in a straight white line behind stiffly drawn-back lips. In the boy's good eye hate shone bright and naked.

Struggling to his feet, Tyrell wavered a moment when again confronting Sinden. He blinked, trying to understand the look of reluctance, of fear mingling with pity and shame on the big man's face. 'It's OK,' he said.

Hump nodded, and something barely discernible seemed to change on his stolid and stubbled countenance. 'I'm sorry,' he muttered, and as Tyrell sent forth his first blow, knocked it easily aside, his own connecting, driving his opponent back to the dirt.

'Get up!' Phil shouted, the toe of his boot enforcing the command. To Hump he yelled, 'Harder, damnit! Harder!'

Tyrell rose unsteadily. Seconds later he was back on the ground. Four times more he went down, the last to lie unmoving.

Phil kicked him, shouted for him to get up. A moment more and he stood over the downed man. Again his boot tested him, and when still it got no reaction, he turned away in disgust. 'Dump some water over him,' he ordered, 'then get him loaded.'

Mike Scobie, grinning toothily, moved to assist Idaho. It took only a few minutes before they had a seemingly dazed Tyrell back in the saddle, hat jammed down on his wet head, gun returned to holster.

'That,' Phil said when they were done, 'was just a sample of what you'll get if ever you come near Bent Arrow or me again.'

Eyes clear and hard as granite, Tyrell gazed down at him in silence.

Phil gestured to Mike Scobie. 'Get him the hell out of here.'

Waiting until Scobie had sent the roan travelling, Roley holstered his gun and spun on Hump who stood with head hung. The flat of his hand cracked hard against the unshaven face.

'Next time you're told to do something, do it! Savvy?' He slapped again, the sound loud, the stinging impact bringing tears to Hump's eyes. 'Don't know why the hell the old man keeps you around. You got less brains than a stinkin' sheep!'

'Don't do that,' Hump howled when again he was struck.

Roley laughed, his hand already in motion. But this time Hump himself was swinging, fist connecting against the side of Farraday's head with such impact that Roley was knocked violently sideways, clear off his feet.

'I said don't do that! I ain't no stinkin' sheep!'

Scobie got to him first, staring down at the inert form, at the open mouth, the rolled-back eyes.

'Sufferin' snakes! I — I think he's dead! I think . . . his neck's broke! Or something!'

His big face a portrait of dismay, of

rapidly growing terror, Hump raised the hand that had done the damage. He stared at it.

'I — I didn't mean it. But he shouldn'ta done what he did. I didn't wanna hurt nobody — but what he said, it warn't right . . . '

Idaho, who'd got down beside Roley said, 'Damn! If I hadn't seen it I'd never've believed it. One lousy clout!'

'What're you saying?' Phil demanded shrilly, gun still trained on Hump, not wanting to look where his brother lay.

'He's dead, is what I'm saying. *Stone cold dead!*'

'Phil,' Hump cried, turning to the younger Farraday, 'I didn't wanna fight that feller. You made me do it, Phil . . . You made me fight him, even when I didn't — '

Twice Phil's gun bucked and belched, hurling the big man backward but not down. Very slowly, as if having trouble fathoming what was happening, Hump's hands rose to his chest.

'Phil . . . it warn't my fault . . . '

Phil squeezed trigger a third time, placing the shot squarely between Hump's eyes.

'How th' hell,' Mike Scobie muttered, 'we gonna explain this to your father when he gets back?'

Struggling to keep the tremor out of his voice, Phil said, 'You saw what happened, both of you.' A now unsteady hand holstered the still smoking pistol. 'You caught Tyrell on our range — brought him in because you suspected him of being involved with recent stock losses. Hump,' he waved shakily to where the man had fallen, 'was nearby . . . ' He hesitated, head slowly bobbing, while he thought out the rest.

When he was through, Scobie's long teeth were showing in a sterile smile. 'Right,' he said. 'An' you had no choice but to shoot the crazy bastard.'

Idaho rose up from his haunches. 'Which is what you should've thought about doing to Tyrell. Because, sure as hell, after what's happened here today, it's what he's bound to do to you.'

The moment Tyrell had been sent on his way, up on the rise west of the ranch buildings a tall figure had risen from the shadows of the cottonwood grove, letting his rifle dangle limply at his side. Stifling a cough, he took a last look at the scene outside the bunkhouse, then turned, retreating deeper into the shadows.

'Good,' he mumbled. 'Nobody kills that bastard but me.'

# 15

He lay on the bed, fully clothed, except for gunbelt and boots, hearing but paying no attention to the Saturday noises out on the streets, the drunken laughter, the occasional yell, the tinny piano-tunes wafting out of a saloon or whorehouse. His body hurt, though not half as much as it might have had Hump not pulled his punches, rocked, rather than pounded him to the ground.

Had he so desired, the man could as easily have killed him. But he'd not wanted to fight, even less to hurt. Maybe Tyrell's readiness to take a beating rather than see him punished had helped, for an unspoken understanding had been communicated, and Tyrell had played along. Farraday boots were responsible for most of his aches, not the fists of the reluctant giant.

The window he'd opened let in a gentle breeze, now slowly growing cold. He ignored it and, while still thinking of Hump Sinden, sleep ambushed him, freeing old and troublesome dreams.

Once again he was at that rail spur, watching the train take on water, a gun tucked behind his belt, hungry, unable to understand how he'd got there . . . A boy trying to remember who he was while visions of leaping, devouring flames, of a screaming woman, kept pushing to the forefront of his mind. Organ music crowded in . . . voices of a man and woman singing. Then nothing but an unknown quantity of time during which he floated in limbo, mind sifting through dense, swirling fog, seeking to snatch back a lost past. Names trickled through his head, and none called back the faintest recollection. He remembered where first he'd seen and adopted the name Tyrell, but not when he'd added the rest of his handle. In a drowsy, dreamlike way he heard himself laugh. It was a hell of a thing when a man didn't even know his own age.

Without warning, darkness, like a powerful undertow, swept him under, drowning him in deep but troublesome sleep.

In Cradlestone's only other saloon, Frank Jelnick was bellied hard up against the bar, the rotgut the dump served doing nothing to improve the sourness of his mood. He'd expected Beresford to get a little sore when, in spite of being warned, he'd again arrived at the back door of the house. This time, though, since he'd put Crowley out of the way, just like the damned shyster had wanted, he'd expected the reception to be better than the last. He'd even hoped to pick up a little more cash for his efforts. What he hadn't expected was the fury that had greeted him.

He poured himself a stiffer drink. It seemed impossible that the lead he'd thrown at the old bugger had missed . . . and yet it somehow had. He

dropped the whiskey down his th.
sleeved his mouth and twisted arou.
scowling at the table where Tickner and
DeVane sat in a huddle, Johnny doing
most of the quiet talking, Len Tickner
simply shaking his head. What, he
wondered, were those two bastards
scheming? Ditching the thought, he
turned back to the bar, back to thinking
about the lawyer.

★　★　★

Marshal Ben Paulson entered the
dining-room pausing briefly to look
around before crossing to where Tyrell,
the only one still there, had just started
on his coffee.

'Exactly what happened at Bent
Arrow?' he asked, hooking out a chair,
dispensing with the preliminaries.

Tyrell put down his cup. 'Why bother
to ask me? Whoever's been talking must
have given you the details.'

'Don't get smart with me, mister.
Yesterday, two men died, and the way I

got it, it was on account of your doing.' Paulson drew a breath, slowly released it. 'Morgan Farraday was in to see me first thing this morning. Claims two of his crew found you on their range. Thinking you could be connected with recent stock losses, they brought you in for his boys to question.' He waited for a reaction. Getting none, his voice tightened. 'Says you got mouthy — poked fun at Hump Sinden and he started beating up on you. Roley tried to stop him, and the big oaf killed him.'

Tyrell's chin lifted a little, eyes narrowing, icing up.

'Right,' Paulson nodded. 'Killed him. The man went crazy, according to those who were there. Only way Phil could stop him was to use his gun. Took three shots to do it.'

'And all in front of witnesses, right?' Tyrell reached for his cup but stopped short of lifting it. 'Going to tell me where I was supposed to be while all this was happening.'

'Told you rode off, right after shooting.'

'You believe it?'

'I'm giving you a chance to tell your side.'

'Then I'll make it short. Farraday, and whoever else fed you that load of buffalo chips, are liars.'

Paulson's face colored. 'That's no explanation.'

'Want me to repeat it?' Tyrell glanced to the right as the waitress advanced toward them. 'You had breakfast?'

★ ★ ★

A while later, still somewhat stiff, a thigh and ribs bruised black and throbbing, Tyrell stood on the sidewalk, building a smoke, thinking of the man called Hump, and why the poor devil had to die. Another question to which he would want an answer.

From somewhere in the vicinity of where he'd seen the new church going up, a bell started clanging, stirring something in a lost canyon of his mind. But, before given any chance to snatch at it, his attention was diverted by a buggy coming steadily down the street. Stretch Norton held the reins. Beside him sat Dana Lane.

They passed without seeing him.

He lit the cigarette, then, after a few moments' deliberation, started off along the planked walk, to where the bell continued its call to the faithful.

It was an old converted building, the church, and, judging from those still passing through the double front doors, well attended. He found a place to wait, smoked, and listened to the organ warming up. About to flick away the butt of the quirly, he spotted a lanky figure treading a path between the vehicles.

'Thinking of going in?' Stretch asked when reaching him, noting the faint marks on Tyrell's face, but making no comment.

'How about you?'

Stretch thumbed back his hat,

averted his face. 'Dana wanted it so
. . . but I figured it best not to.' Lifting
his gaze, he added with quiet signifi-
cance, 'Leastways, not for the present.'

Tyrell hesitated before responding
with a slow nod. Then: 'Denver alone at
the ranch?'

'Him and the cook.' A small jerk of
Norton's head indicated the church.
'His idea. Dana's never missed a
service. And . . . well, you try arguing
with that old rooster. Anyway, wouldn't
be a good day for unwelcome visitors.
Not the way those two've got themselves organized.' He cocked an
eyebrow. 'Something on your mind?'

Tyrell told him of the idea he'd been
kicking around.

'Got curious about them water holes
myself, soon after I got here,' the lanky
Cross bar A hand said when he was
through. 'Way Nat had it figured,
they're partly fed from some catchment
up in the hills, though we've never
been able to find it. Leastways, not
on horseback.' He shrugged absently.

'None of us were anxious for rock climbing, so we left it there.'

'Get a lot of rain this way.'

'Sometimes. But there's also been long dry spells. Which's what had Nat reasoning that whatever's underground is fed mainly from a river or lake that could be miles — a whole heap of them — from here. It's about the only thing that would account for the holes and seeps regularly topping up.'

'Might also account for the sounds of thunder for which the valley's named.' Tyrell looked around, almost as if expecting to hear the rumbling once more. 'Heard it briefly when I was up in those hills. But not all that loud.'

'Yeah, seems almost to be fading away.'

'What I heard,' Tyrell said, 'sounded more like an earth tremor than thunder.'

'Which accounts for Nat's thinking. Every so often the flow would come in one hell of a rush, probably creating echoes when passing through caves or tunnels, or whatever its route consists of. As it fills it sends its overflow upward.'

And could be, thought Tyrell, over the years the caverns have changed shape, broadened or broken up, reducing the volume of the rumbling, thunderlike sound. He turned so that he was facing east.

'Travels all the way to Bent Arrow, right?'

'And beyond. But the flow appears to slow down as it moves easterly, so Farraday gets a lot less.'

'Maybe his reason for wanting to own the Cross bar A.'

'Possible. Though it doesn't make all that much sense. He's sunk a few wells — got windmills put up, water piped to other watering points.' Staring in the direction of the Farraday spread, his head moved negatively. 'No, I reckon he's got water enough for all his needs, and maybe then some.'

★   ★   ★

Tyrell was almost at the livery barn when a slight figure stepped nervously into his path.

'Tyrell?'

He looked down at the small-framed man he'd seen out at Jelnick's 7-Bar, the one who'd made a point of keeping to the sidelines. 'You already know that.'

Len Tickner's narrow head bobbed quickly. 'Right . . . '

'Want something?'

'Well . . . ' Tickner's narrow shoulders performed a fast shrug. 'Depends on how bad you want to find out what's been happenin' to Cross bar A beef — an' that rider that got himself killed.'

# 16

It had been a bad night for Eli Cradock. Whiskey had helped put him to sleep, but in the early hours of Sunday morning another bout of coughing had forced him out of bed. He felt weaker than he'd ever felt, doubtful that he had strength enough to lift himself from the rickety chair in which he was slumped.

From the hotel window he watched the two riders moving out of his range of vision: Tyrell and a smaller man. He started a quiet, bitter curse that was cut short when another tight, dry scratchiness heaved up from his lungs, tore at his throat, doubling him over in another seemingly endless coughing spell. Gasping for air, he stared at the blood-speckled phlegm caught in the already much-soiled handkerchief. Time was running out. He knew that.

Just as he knew that somehow, in some way, he'd hold on, at least long enough to see that son of a bitch go down in front of his gun.

★ ★ ★

They'd been riding for over a half-hour, neither speaking, when abruptly Len Tickner twisted around in his saddle.

'Thought we'd come to an arrangement?' he queried, and got back nothing. Hooded eyes blinked. 'So when do I see some cash?'

'Soon as you give me something worthwhile.' Tyrell tapped his waist in a manner that hinted at a moneybelt under his shirt. 'I've got it. You just make sure you deliver.'

Tickner blinked again, tongue flicking at dry lips. 'I will. Don't sweat over that.'

'I'm not. Because if you're stringing me along, you'll not be making any return ride. And that's a promise not to take lightly.'

Len Tickner swallowed, shifted uneasily. 'It'll be worth it, you'll see. Like I told you, I been wantin' out for a long time. Just been too scared to quit Jelnick an' DeVane. But — but after what I seen you do to Johnny . . . ' He broke off, scraped a gloved hand across his mouth. 'Also, to make a clean break, 'til I find other work. I need a few bucks to tide me over.'

No more was said until, when morning was well done, they arrived where brush almost hid the start of the narrow trail.

'Mister,' Tyrell said softly when Tickner turned to make sure he was still following, 'this better not be some game you're playing. I've already been here — and you know it. There's nothing down there but a roofless shack.'

Tickner's head shook vigorously.

'No. You just never knew where to look — what to look for.'

Tyrell shrugged. 'It's your play.'

'You'll see.' Tickner touched spurs to his mount.

In the hillside pocket the silence was almost deafening, broken only by occasional inquiring sounds of rock-dwelling insects. Tyrell hauled up to the right of the smaller man, gaze scouring the restricted terrain. Then, suddenly he was moving, swinging down from the roan, grabbing Tickner as he moved, jerking him out of saddle, dumping him heavily on to his back.

'Go!' he yelled, and with instant response the horse wheeled sharply, lunging toward the far edge of the clearing. By then Tyrell had Tickner jerked back to his feet, gun barrel pressed hard against his head. 'Tell whoever's back there to show them-selves — else you'll be suffering brain damage!'

Stiffening under the pressure of the Colt's muzzle, Tickner's bellow was a sick, squealing sound. 'Johnny — don't! Johnny . . . '

Rocks and scrubby growth east of the

tumbling-down shack provided greater scope for concealment, and it was from there Tyrell had expected any ambush to come. Instead, it arrived from the opposite side, in the form of the redheaded DeVane appearing as if from nowhere, gun levelled and already firing murderously. Almost lost in the racket came violent and abusive profanity, the panicked whinny of Tickner's horse as it ploughed away.

The small man yelped fearfully when Tyrell plunged him to the ground, released him and rolled over on to his side, knifelike pain stabbing through bruised thigh when lifting upward again, his own gun spitting its deadly response to the attack.

Mouth gaping as he was thrown into a backward stumble, Johnny DeVane's eyes dropped to the gun in his hand, feeling it grow terribly heavy, watching in stupefaction as it dragged his arm down. A fast-misting gaze lifted to where Tyrell stood, then it was as if an invisible hand was forcing him down into darkness.

'Jelnick!' Tyrell called. 'Show your face!'

'He's not here,' Tickner whined from where he lay. 'It — it was all Johnny's idea.' Slowly lifting himself to an elbow, he flicked a nervous glance toward the shack. 'He made me do it,' he almost blubbered. 'Swore to kill me if I didn't do like he said!'

'And he damn near did,' Tyrell snarled, reaching down to lift the man's gun from its holster, letting the barrel of his own dip menacingly. 'Get up.'

'No!' Tickner howled, cringing into a fetus-like position. 'Please! — *don't!* I had to do it! I was scared of Johnny. He — he was a little crazy. You — you just seen what he did . . .'

'I said get up,' Tyrell repeated, and waited until Tickner was standing before him, trembling. 'Now let's hear it all.'

'I — I told you. Johnny — he fancied himself as a fast gun. Couldn't take it when you made him look stupid in front of Frank an' me. He — he had to get even. It — it was eating at him.'

'Why here?'

Tickner dragged the back of his glove under his nose. 'He — he figured no one'd ever find you here — no one'd ever look.'

'And Jelnick?'

The smaller man's head shook. 'He — he never knew. Might've guessed — but he wasn't part of it. It was all Johnny.'

'But he was part of the kid from Cross bar A getting killed.'

Tickner made another pass at his nose. 'I — I guess,' he sniffed. 'But he never said nothing to us about it. He . . . he's got a deal going with someone.' His head jerked up sharply. 'No — I don't know who's been paying him, an' that's the bare-ass truth. It was some kinda secret me an' Johnny wasn't let in on.'

The Colt's barrel made a meaningful shift.

'That's it — everything I know. Him

and Frank, they always met secretly. But it's got to be someone important, 'cause Frank said if the deal came off we'd stand to make a packet.'

'Jelnick also the one who shot up Denver Crowley?' Tyrell asked, believing Tickner at that moment to be too terrified to lie.

'Could be . . . He — he was gone most of the night it happened. S'posed to've seen the one who's been giving him his orders. All I know's he came back long after midnight, with money an' a couple of bottles.'

'What about Nat Anderson?'

This time Tickner's delay was longer. 'Yeah,' he mumbled, dropping his gaze. 'That was him. Him an' Johnny. That's how I know, on account of Johnny liked to talk. Had to spill it to someone — brag how they done it so's it looked like an accident.'

'How about the rustling?'

'Jelnick,' came the softly muttered reply. 'Ever since setting up here he's been lifting stock, not just from the

Anderson spread, but from all over the valley. Most he sells to the mines up north.'

'I'm going to ask this just once,' Tyrell told him, thumbing back the Colt's hammer. 'Who's Jelnick working for?'

Tickner backed away, snake eyes stretched to their limit.

'No! Don't! If I knew I'd tell you. But I swear to God, I don't!'

Tyrell studied him, then, nodding, dropped the Colt back into its holster.

With Tickner's and DeVane's guns stashed in one of his saddlebags, he collected the redhead's horse from where it had been hobbled in a niche dug into the cliff back of the shack, gathered up the reins of Tickner's mount, and stepped aboard the roan. Tickner moved towards his dun, but Tyrell's voice fetched him up short.

'Remember what I said would happen if you were stringing me along?'

'You're crazy! You can't leave me here! It's miles from anywhere!'

'Planned a little worse for me, didn't you?' Tyrell smiled down at him. 'Besides, you might want to get your friend planted.'

Tickner moved still further away. 'For God's sake, man . . . '

'What I might do,' Tyrell said, 'is give you one last chance to tell the rest of it.'

'I can't! Damnit to hell! How many times I got to tell you? I honest to God don't know any more!'

Tyrell waited, watching fear grow wild in his face. Then, swinging back to the ground, said, 'Help me get your partner loaded.'

Tickner gawked. 'You're . . . taking him into town?'

'Nope. The 7-Bar. Figure Jelnick may want to lend a hand with the burying.'

★ ★ ★

Sunday morning, and sick of being cooped up, Flo trod the boardwalks of Cradlestone, ignoring the inquisitive glances of townsfolk also about, particularly those using the main street on their way home from church. As she walked she remembered a time when she'd been able to enter any establishment, purchase whatever she desired, charging it to Nat Anderson's account.

She was looking into the window of the mercantile, recalling the day she'd bought two dresses there, one of which had only just been put on display, when, in the glass she caught the reflection of someone a short distance behind her. Startled, she heeled about.

Before her stood a plump, round-faced individual with a carefully waxed moustache. He raised his derby, revealing a bald head.

'A pleasure to see you again, Flo.'

# 17

'Lloyd . . . ' Flo gasped, fear echoing in the sounding of his name.

'That's right, Flo. Lloyd Gaynor.' The man smiled broadly. 'Quite a surprise, seeing you step off the stage. Never figured on ever seeing you again. Not after you and Burt . . . left Wichita.'

'What do you want?' she asked, hand at painted mouth.

'Well, now . . . I thought a little talk in private might be nice. It's Sunday, and since the saloon's closed 'til this afternoon, and I've some time off . . . '

Words not intended for delicate ears hissed forth from the woman's compressed lips. But, some fifteen minutes later, they were seated in the front room of the small house, Lloyd Gaynor assuring her that he'd been careful not to have anyone see him going there. He looked again at the closed door leading to the rest of the house.

'Sure it's only you home?'

'I already told you the boy's out,' she snapped, stopping just short of adding *again*. 'Now what the hell is it you want?'

His gaze slid back to her. 'You've changed, Flo. When I saw you arrive, I wasn't sure I was looking at the same woman.'

'What the hell do you want?' she demanded again, voice as tight as a bow string.

'Well,' Gaynor made an open-handed gesture, 'let's say it sort of set me on my heels, learning you're the — ah — widow of the late Nathaniel Anderson, an' probable heir to his property. Especially since the last time I saw you you'd just spliced up with that no-good Burt Castell, who tended bar with me. Thing that troubles me, Flo, is the fact that you had no kid then. And even if old Burt later gave you one' — his smile stretched — 'he'd be nowhere near the age of the squirt you've got tagging along.'

'*What the hell do you want?*'

'Depends,' Lloyd said, contemplatively stroking his smoothly shaven chin. 'How much do you figure to make on this deal?'

The woman looked hard into his pudgy face.

'Lloyd,' she said, 'you were never half as smart as you thought yourself to be.'

'But,' he grinned, 'smart enough to know what they call women who marry again while still married to another man.'

A deathly hush descended upon the room, lifting only when Flo's frost-bitten voice asked, 'This some kind of shakedown?'

'Flo, Flo,' he soothed, head shaking. 'How could you think such a thing? Let's rather call it a sharing of good fortune.'

At the far side of the room the brass doorknob again silently turned, and the door moved back into its frame.

Neither had heard it open. Neither heard it close.

\* \* \*

Arrangements for Roley's burial completed, Morgan Farraday remained undecided about making the ride home. With him, seated in silence at a table in the Jack O' Diamonds, were Phil and Idaho Smith, each entertaining his own private thoughts. After refilling his glass, Farraday shoved the bottle to the center of the table, inviting the others to help themselves.

'Still don't understand how you could just let him ride away,' he grunted.

'All happened too fast,' Idaho replied, bottle in hand. 'It's like Phil told you. We were too interested in trying to help Roley to notice he'd grabbed his bronc and skedaddled.'

Farraday shifted his gaze. 'This's all straight goods?'

Phil hesitated. 'You sound as if you

don't believe me . . . '

'Not that at all,' his father returned impatiently, swallowing half his drink. 'Want to be absolutely sure, that's all — and that tomorrow you tell it the same way to the coroner.'

'It's exactly like Phil's told you,' Idaho said. 'There's nothing to worry about. He was forced to kill that crazy bastard.'

'Then,' said Farraday, his tone heavily frosted, 'the way I see it, he's responsible for everything that happened.'

'Sure as hell was,' Idaho agreed.

Farraday retreated back into silence, mind focused on the report Doc Halyard would present at the inquest. He couldn't remember the name the medico had ascribed to the cause of Roley's death, but it wasn't a broken neck. Something to do with the brain being badly jarred, maybe even dislodged. The same sort of damage, Halyard had explained, that a blow from a heavy club could cause. But what the hell did it matter how Roley'd died? His first-born was dead, and all because of . . .

'All right,' he said abruptly, stretching across the table for the bottle. 'If Tyrell's responsible for Roley and that idiot Sinden dying, then he's got to be made to pay.' His gaze settled upon Idaho. 'You as good as you claim?'

Smith's lips pulled downward in an affirmative smile.

'All right, then here's how you can pick up an easy two hundred.' Farraday's voice dropped to a menacing growl. 'Kill the mangy son of a bitch. But do it for people to see — witnesses to say it was on the square.' He glanced around the saloon, still near-empty that early in the afternoon. 'Right here, or out in the street, would be a good place.'

Idaho chuckled quietly. 'Consider it a done deal.'

'Unless,' Phil put in quietly, head making a short jerk toward the batwings, 'the law has something to say.'

Eyes turned to Ben Paulson on his way to their table. When he stopped, Morgan Farraday gave him no chance to speak.

'Well? What've you done about my boy's death?'

'Nothing I can do. According to the account given by Phil and him' — a twitch of Paulson's head indicated Smith — 'Tyrell pulled no trigger, laid no hand on Roley. It also happened out of town — which's out of my jurisdiction, a fact of which you've more than once reminded me.'

'Then get the hell out of my sight,' the boss of Bent Arrow growled, 'and let me ensure that justice gets done.'

'Mr Farraday, there's still to be an inquest. Don't — '

The rancher's scowl cut him short. 'You still here?'

'What about Sinden?' Paulson asked through stiffened lips. 'Told you've ordered him buried at county expense.'

'You heard it right,' Idaho grinned. 'You expect the boss to pay for burying the one who murdered his own son?'

'I wasn't talking to you,' Paulson snapped.

Smith shot up out of his chair, but Farraday's command held him in check. 'Sit down,' he growled, and returning his attention to Paulson, asked: 'Anything else you want?'

Paulson, face darkening, thrust a final glare at Farraday's hired gun, turned and walked away.

A while later, the bottle not quite dead, Farraday hitched back his chair.

'The hell with wasting time, sitting around this dump. Let's get on home, come back for the inquest tomorrow.'

★ ★ ★

Tyrell was about decided that it had been a poor idea, electing to wait until Jelnick returned from wherever he was.

They'd arrived at 7-Bar by mid-afternoon and found it deserted.

Leaving DeVane's body in a small shed adjoining the barn, where it could wait until Jelnick and Tickner got around to digging a hole for it, he'd searched the house for weapons. Along with an old 12-gauge Greener, a Sharps in fairly good condition, and a Winchester minus a loading-lever, whatever ammunition had been around was now in a place where he could keep an eye on them. Then he'd settled down to wait.

But now, with clouds bunching darkly together, cold setting in, the approach of night was increasing Tickner's nervousness.

'Want more coffee?' he asked, moving to light a lamp.

Tyrell glanced at the tin cup parked on the arm of the dilapidated chair in which he slouched, and shook his head. He considered telling him to get a fire started, but changed his mind. To do so the little man would have to fetch wood from outside.

'Could be,' Tickner said, refitting the lamp's badly sooted chimney, 'he won't be back. Sometimes — sometimes he's away for days, depending on what he's got going.' When Tyrell failed to comment, he asked, 'You . . . figuring on staying all night?'

It was a question Tyrell was asking himself while looking around the room in which the lamp's yellow glow assembled dismal, depressing shadows. With boxes and empty sacks piled in corners, bundles of harness and ropes either waiting to be repaired or dumped, a saddle no longer worth two dollars, and old ashes clogging the fireplace, the place was a lazy rat's nest. The furniture, what there was of it, no better than the rest of the junk.

Worse was the fetor of human sweat, unwashed clothing, ancient cooking and burnt grease smells, blending with those of stale wood and cigarette smoke, hanging like a miasma in the air, permeating everything. Turning his back on it would be a pleasure.

He stood up, pain jolting down his bruised thigh. Tickner was probably right; waiting could be a total waste of time. But the ride to Cradlestone was a long one, and each minute the night grew colder. The ride to Cross bar A, though, was not as long . . .

On the verge of ditching his original intentions of waiting for Frank Jelnick and squeezing some truth out of him at gunpoint, he recalled the expression on Stretch Norton's face when he'd told of Dana wanting him to accompany her to the church service.

Tickner, as if recognizing his indecision, started to say something, but whatever he'd planned was cancelled when the faint drumming of hoofbeats reached them. Quickly he crossed to the window, drew aside the burlap being used as a curtain, and peered out into the rapidly spreading dark.

'Someone coming,' he whispered needlessly.

'Good,' Tyrell said quietly, unsheathing the Colt. 'Now you go and sit down' — he indicated the chair he'd recently vacated — 'and keep very quiet.'

# 18

Just when it began to seem as if it was taking Jelnick too long to put away his horse, his booted feet came thudding across the yard, approaching the back of the house.

'Johnny? Len?' he boomed the instant the kitchen door opened.

'In here,' Tickner croaked at a signal from Tyrell.

Jelnick stomped into the room, glancing quickly about when finding Tickner seated stiffly, fingers biting into the chair's worn leather-covered arms. 'Where's Johnny? And who the hell's horse's that in the — ?'

'Touch that gun,' Tyrell warned, stepping from the shadows, 'and it'll be the last thing you do!'

'What the hell is this?' Jelnick scowled, squinting into the gloom, lifting his hands to shoulder level. 'Still looking for strays?'

'Not any more. Got what I came for. The yellow-bellied louse who killed Nat Anderson and young Henkel . . . who tried to do the same for Denver Crowley.'

His throat a thing constricted, gaze fastened hard upon Tyrell moving into view, closer to Jelnick, Tickner loosened his grip on the chair, letting his hands fall into his lap.

A baffled expression twisted Jelnick's hairy face.

'You crazy? Anderson had an accident; nobody killed him!'

Tyrell tossed a small sideways nod to where Tickner sat.

'Not what your partner says. Says you and DeVane fixed it to look like one. Told me also about Henkel and Crowley.'

Rage washed away the bafflement, but before Jelnick could say anything, Tickner blurted, 'I had to Frank! I had to! The son of a bitch was gonna kill me — same's he did Johnny!'

For a handful of seconds Jelnick went on glaring at Tickner. Then, hands still raised, he made a gesture of defeat.

'OK, so now you know. What're you going to do? Kill me too?'

'No, that's a chore the law can handle.'

'Yeah?' Jelnick's laugh was quiet, sneering. 'It's a long way back to town, bucko. A lot could happen along the way.'

'Uh-huh. Like you telling me who's been giving you your orders.'

Jelnick began another laugh, hands starting to lower themselves as his eyes darted briefly about the clammy-cold room.

'Keep them up,' Tyrell snapped. 'All the way up. Then turn around.'

With a shrug of resignation, Jelnick obeyed, allowing the gun to be lifted from his holster.

Tyrell took a step back, ordering the bearded man to put his hands behind his back, intending to have Tickner do the tying.

His gaze never leaving them, Tickner eased himself a little further to the edge of the chair, at the same time slipping a knife from beneath the cuff of his left sleeve.

Jelnick was already dropping his hands when Tyrell heard the shrill intake of breath, the rush of movement. Wheeling sharply, he caught the image of the small, blurred figure lunging at him, the dull flash of light on steel and, just as hard as he could, swung the gun taken from Jelnick.

He heard Tickner scream, the knife clatter to the floor. The next moment a larger, heavier body was barrelling into him, slamming him off his feet with such force both guns he'd been holding were jarred from his grasp. Above him Jelnick uttered a deep curse; somewhere else Tickner howled painfully. Then Jelnick was suddenly lifting his weight, swearing.

Tyrell rolled over, from the corner of an eye saw Jelnick crouched, hands frantically sweeping the floor in search of the lost weapons. His own hands scraped the uneven wood.

Jelnick's fingers connected with something that shifted under their touch. He swore again, made another grab, another more triumphant sound, and snatched up the thin, long-bladed knife Tickner had tried to use. Pushing himself up on to his knees he drew back his right arm, started the knife in a downward plunge to where he could see Tyrell rolling on to his back . . . and let loose a scream that was a fusion of fear and frustrated fury. Desperately, with every ounce of power he could muster, he tried to bring the knife down. But, as if somehow the eyes that stared at the upswinging barrel of a Colt had severed mental communication, the muscles in his arm became totally paralyzed. With a sound neither animal nor human, he tried to move from the path of the flame already blazing at him, and instead felt his head almost jerked from his body.

'Damnit,' Tickner howled, 'my arm's broke — you busted it! How the hell d'you expect me to ride like this? At night — with the weather coming up bad!' Tenderly he caressed the arm secured between crude splints, suspended in an equally crude rope sling.

'Your choice. Far as I'm concerned you can stay here and wait for the law. Or — ' Straightening, Tyrell took the long-bladed knife from where he'd dumped it on the fire-place mantel. He'd been careless, underestimating the man's cunning when leaving him alone, even for so short a time, to brew the coffee. ' — you can use this and save the county the expense of a hanging.' He let the knife drop into Tickner's lap, eliciting a startled yelp — a grab at the damaged arm, and more agonized whining.

'I told you! I never killed no one! It was Frank and Johnny — never me!' Hate glistening in narrow, watery eyes,

Tickner glared up at him. 'Son of a bitch! Haven't you got any feelings?'

'For you — not a one.'

'Where — where you going?'

Tyrell stopped on his way through to the rear of the house. He turned, frowning. 'Why should that concern you? You're not coming along.'

★   ★   ★

Lloyd Gaynor took the night's takings up to the office and living-quarters of the saloon's owner, bid him goodnight, went back downstairs, killed the last of the lights, and left by the back door. The night was cold and without a moon. What he could see of the sky held the threat of rain. He shrugged, pocketed the key, turned up his collar, pulled his hat down tightly, and started walking.

It had been a mite busier than most Sundays, possibly because of interest in the inquest scheduled for the next day. But, overall, just another quiet Sunday night. Not that he was complaining. He had more on his mind than the number of drinks he'd dispensed.

Until now he'd had no reason to give any thought to the total value of the Anderson estate, but, on reflection, considering the size of the Cross bar A, the number of years old Anderson had held title to it . . . He chuckled silently. Any way you looked at it, it had to be worth a good chunk of cold cash.

Continuing along the unlit back street that would eventually bring him to the rooming-house he called home, Gaynor's thoughts returned to the woman called Flo. Without realizing it, his head was shaking in quiet amusement, remembering her as once she'd been. She could have had her choice of suckers back then, but instead she'd taken up with that two-bit Burt Castell. Hell, everyone recognized Castell for what he was — a handsome, silver-tongued phony. But not Flo.

Only when already well into one of the narrower alleys that shortened his walk home did Gaynor get the feeling that he was not alone. He stopped, slowly turning, eyes nervously probing the dark, certain he'd heard trailing footsteps. An iciness touched his spine and suddenly he was seized by an irrational urge to run, to be where there was plenty of light. His feet, though, felt as if they'd become fossilized.

'Gaynor?' a voice called softly. 'Wait up. I have something important to discuss.'

'Who is it?' he queried, voice wheezy, shaky.

The footsteps drew closer, moving a little faster, and now he could see part of the darkness take on distinctive human form.

'Who is it?' he repeated, and even as the question was asked his nostrils detected a cologne not likely to be used by the local barber. For a moment he breathed easier, then again asked, 'Who — who is it? What do you want?'

Instead of a reply, there came a soft, whooshing sound an instant before something hard and unyielding struck down at him, creating a volcanic eruption inside his skull. A scarlet brilliance flared up behind his eyes, the derby bounced off his shoulder, toppling to the dirt, and his knees turned to water. He was already going down when the second blow was struck, and on the ground when a third strike opened the back of his skull.

A pity Jelnick, that damned incompetent, could not have removed Denver Crowley that easy . . . But, no matter. Much as he'd have preferred him permanently out of the way, there was a means by which he could use the law to control the old fool.

With the dead barman's pockets turned inside out, Vance Beresford withdrew from one of his own a large white handkerchief, carefully wiped his hands, then turned and pointed himself back the way he had come, the silver-knobbed walking-cane held unobtrusively at his side.

Like a beast that had been lying in

ambush, a sharp gust of wind lashed at him when he stopped out of the alley, rapidly lifting to gale force before the distance of a block had been travelled, buffering doors and windows, turning street surfaces into swirling, stinging clouds of dust.

# 19

The inquest took less than thirty minutes. Cradlestone's mayor who, when so called upon, performed the duties of district coroner, shunted through a verdict of death resulting from violent assault, in the case of Roland Farraday, and justifiable homicide, insofar as Hump Sinden's demise was concerned, thus entirely exonerating Phil Farraday of any guilt.

Morgan Farraday, though in no mood for celebration, put up one more round of drinks before taking his leave of his son, Idaho Smith and the grinning Mike Scobie.

Outside the Jack O' Diamonds he paused to once more contemplate the trail of damage left by Sunday night's blast. Several windows which had lost their glass were now boarded up, garbage, leaves, small branches and an assortment of other junk that couldn't be nailed down lay caught up in small heaps along the sides of the boardwalk. In at least two places he could see where wooden awnings had been torn apart, and elsewhere, people were still trying to sweep out dust, restore their premises to some semblance of what they'd been.

He stepped off the walk, his mouth a tight, twisting line. It was not only the town that had suffered damage. Bent Arrow had also been a casualty. Not only had the house, the barn, and blacksmith shop been left in need of repairs, but, just before leaving for the inquest, a rider had come in to report that two of his windmills had been wrecked.

Were he a superstitious man, Morgan Farraday might have accepted it as an omen. But he was not, and so he shouldered aside such thoughts. But what he was still having difficulty removing was the smiling image of his late wife . . . the expression on Helena's face whenever she'd been proved right, whenever he'd gone against her counsel.

He continued along his chosen route, no longer seeing anything to distract him from his thoughts, oblivious to those who, in passing, offered respectful greetings.

Not long later, he was standing stone-faced in Vance Beresford's office.

'Thought you'd have been at the inquest,' he growled.

On his side of the desk, Beresford shrugged heavy shoulders, allowed his heavy frown to melt.

'Something came up. Anyway . . . the verdict was entirely predictable, wasn't it?'

'And why not?' Farraday glowered. Then, somewhat more calmly: 'Funeral's this afternoon. You coming?'

'I'll do my best,' the lawyer promised with small intent, his mind centered elsewhere. 'Right now I'm . . . ' Allowing whatever he was going to say to float, he said, 'I saw Judge Thackery this morning. He's put his conclusions, favoring Flo Anderson and her son's claims, in writing. But he still insists upon sending them to the county seat for ratification.'

'And? You expect the girl to contest it?'

Beresford shook his head. 'I told you; she can't afford to. However, there are other considerations . . . '

'What the hell do you mean — *other* considerations?' Farraday snarled, remembering Flo Anderson's last remarks when he'd called upon her. 'We had an agreement!'

'No, Morgan . . . you merely assumed we did.'

'Why, you dirty — !'

Farraday's hand was already upon the butt of his gun when Beresford said, 'Go ahead. That's sure to get you somewhere.' His lips quirked coldly. 'You shouldn't have lied to me, Morgan — shouldn't have told me your only reason for wanting Cross bar A was for expansion. Not when, depending on circumstances, it could mean the death or survival of Bent Arrow. Or,' he went on slowly, 'a way for you to gain absolute control of the entire valley.'

He waited for comment, and when still Farraday kept his mouth clamped shut, indicated the chair on the other side of the desk. 'Sit down. This might take a while.'

'I'll stand,' the rancher growled.

'Suit yourself.' Resuming his seat, Beresford leaned back, his smile still totally devoid of humor. 'Your anxiety to possess the Anderson spread got me curious, Morgan. More so when suddenly you, of all people, have a guest at your place — one you're very careful to keep in seclusion. I'm talking, of course, about the geologist you brought in — the one you'd have everyone believe was a friend from the East, out here for health reasons.'

White showed around Farraday's flared nostrils. 'How the hell do you know all this?'

'Because of another mistake you

made. You knew the man had a drinking problem — which is probably another reason you kept him away from town. But, when he departed, what you should also have done was accompany him. At least as far as the next town — as I did.'

The question was there, blazing in Farraday's eyes, but he refused to ask it.

'No, not on the stage from here. With you and your boys to see Metcalf off, that would have been foolish. No . . . much as I'd have preferred that mode of travel, I used a horse instead. Rode up to the first way station, where I met and boarded the stage. After that it was a simple matter of getting acquainted with Mr Amery Metcalf — even more so in the first saloon he could find.'

'You — slimy son-of-a-bitch!' Farraday hissed.

Beresford chuckled softly. 'In this instance, rather than take offense, I'll merely consider the source.'

'So you got him drunk, and he spilled

his guts. That still — '

'Allow me to finish,' Beresford said, raising a silencing hand. 'Your friend Metcalf, as it transpired, was more than just glad to be putting miles between himself and Bent Arrow. To put it mildly, Morgan, he did not find you a very gracious or tolerant host. But,' he shrugged, 'that's of no importance. What is immensely so, is what his survey revealed. About the lake or reservoir under Cross bar A — from which your operation draws the bulk of its water.'

'What the hell is this? A scheme to hold me to ransom?'

The question reached Beresford's ears almost like an echo of the one he'd heard fired at Lloyd Gaynor, when he'd stood at the door listening in on him and the woman still calling herself Florence Anderson.

'We'll get to that when I'm through,' he said. 'By then you'll have a much better appreciation of your position — and your need. You see, Metcalf told me about the thing you suspected and feared — the weakness of Bent Arrow, which his survey confirmed. What he told me was that all your water, other than that derived from rain — which is far too infrequent for the continuing prosperity of anyone in the valley — comes from a single tributary from that underground reservoir. He told me, also — ' Again there was a pause, but this time not punctuated by any smile. ' — that by the simple act of damming up one of the smallest water holes — *on Cross bar A land*, I should add — the flow to Bent Arrow, and elsewhere, would be shut off. And all it would require would be a couple of strategically placed sticks of dynamite.'

Farraday's quiet laugh was brimmed with scorn.

'You were dealing with a drunk! He could've told you any damned thing that came to mind, just as long as you kept buying the drinks.'

'A poor try,' Beresford said, returning to his feet. 'You see, after Metcalf passed out in his hotel room, I searched it. Found the book in which he'd recorded all his survey and research notes.'

For a long while silence weighed heavy in the lawyer's office. Farraday flicked a glance at the safe standing in a corner.

'It's not there,' Beresford smiled. 'So get rid of that idea.'

With the release of his breath Farraday's shoulders slumped.

'Let's hear the rest.'

'It's like this, Morgan. I've been contacted by a Chicago-based syndicate, an operation buying up ranchland for British investors. They've made a tentative but far more attractive offer than you have. So, what it boils down to is this. Either you match, or better it, or the valley acquires a new boss.'

Again silence reigned. Then, in a voice drawn tight, Farraday asked, 'What's their bid?'

The answer almost had his jaw dropping.

'Damn you! That's an insane price! It would take every cent I have — and I'd still need to borrow to afford it!'

'But,' smiled Beresford, 'think of what you'd have to gain.'

Farraday did. 'All right, you lousy bastard, you've got me over a barrel. But if this doesn't pan out, you'll wish you were back wherever the hell you came from!' Then, as if another thought had just been born full-grown, he glared murderously at Cradlestone's only lawyer. 'You lousy, scheming bastard! This — this syndicate . . . They never contacted you! *You're it!* Or a big part of it!'

This time amusement was more than evident in Beresford's smile.

'That would only be good business, wouldn't it?'

Jaw clenched, blunt beard jutting, Farraday heaved himself up to full height.

'Beresford,' he breathed, 'if ever I were to lose all I've worked and sweated for . . . that's the day they'll be nailing down the lid on your coffin.' He wheeled about, pausing at the door. 'Keep that in mind, because I never make hollow promises!'

Beresford chuckled softly, contentedly, when the door closed. But within the blink of an eye he was back to thinking about Lloyd Gaynor . . .

Never a man to fully believe in coincidence, Beresford was again forced to give thought to it, for nothing else he knew of could explain his arrival at Flo Anderson's door precisely when he had. Nor the fact that a man's voice had lifted, penetrating the wood just as he was about to knock. Or the words heard . . . sufficient to have him ease the door open an inch, to hear enough in order to know the man had become a threat that would have to be removed. And this time he could not use Frank Jelnick.

By ten that morning he'd picked up enough from talk on the streets to know Gaynor's body had been discovered, that robbery was believed to have been the motive for the attack. Except for a gold ring which would have been difficult to remove from the chubby finger, the body had been stripped of everything valuable.

Beresford harbored no concern regarding Gaynor's death. The man was a nonentity. A stupid and greedy little nothing. What did give him cause for worry was what he'd overheard in that house.

If Farraday were to learn anything of it, were anyone to find out why Lloyd Gaynor had to die, the entire scheme to gain ownership of Cross bar A, and ultimately control of Trueno Valley, would collapse like a house of cards.

Cursing the henna-haired woman, he bit off the end of a cigar, fumbled in a drawer for matches.

Voices from the sidewalk brought him out of his chair and to the window. Peering up the street he saw the man called Tyrell reining toward the marshal's office. Hunched in the saddle, one of Frank Jelnick's cohorts rode at his left. Two led horses trailed behind, each carrying a slicker-wrapped bundle.

In his stomach, part of Beresford's breakfast turned slowly over, and the still-gray sky seemed to lose a little of its weak light.

# 20

Doctored and jailed, Len Tickner continued his whining pleas of innocence, offering to swear on a stack of Bibles that he'd been nothing but low man on the totem pole, that Jelnick and DeVane seldom let him in on their plans.

Paulson left him in a cell and returned to the front office.

'Still singing the same song?' Tyrell frowned from where he was slacked out in a hardback chair.

Paulson nodded, taking his place behind the desk. 'So Miss Lane was right. Her uncle's death was no accident.'

Tyrell took the makings from a shirt pocket, said nothing.

'Thing is,' Paulson muttered a little angrily, 'we know how it was done, who did it, but still not who paid to have it done.'

'Could make a guess,' Tyrell said, fingers curving a paper. 'It's no secret who's been wanting the Anderson spread.'

Paulson gave it brief thought, then a slow but worried nod.

'Yeah . . . Farraday.'

'He's got the money to buy guns . . . and killings.' But even as he said it Tyrell's mind was moving in another direction.

Shaking his head when the tobacco and papers were offered, Paulson let his gaze swing to the door leading to the cell block.

'I'd best get someone from the records office to take his statement — get it properly witnessed so it'll hold up in court. With that arm broken he can't sign anything.' He tossed a long glance through the street window, brought it back to the weary face of Tyrell. 'You look like hell.'

'Feel like it.' Tyrell smiled bleakly. 'Planned to ride in last night, but the weather turned bad. Spent most of the time watching that little runt.' He drew deeply on the quirly, let smoke dribble from his nostrils. 'Don't turn your back on him.'

'Going to charge him for trying to knife you?'

'Guess not.' Unfolding himself from the chair, Tyrell felt the throb in his leg start again. 'Probably be moving on soon. Don't care to spend time in any court.'

His answer brought a slight narrowing to the marshal's eyes.

'Heard him squawking for a lawyer,' Tyrell said. 'Seems to know his way around.'

Paulson leaned back, still undecided about the man standing before him. 'Probably remembers when DeVane was jugged on a drunk and disorderly. Instead of getting the six months he deserved, some . . . shyster got him off with a miserable little fine.'

The cigarette paused inches from Tyrell's lips. 'He still in town, this lawyer?'

* * *

The hotel room was still bathed in the afternoon's gray light when Tyrell opened his eyes, not sure how long he'd slept, nor why he'd woken, thinking of the henna-haired woman.

Shouldering up against the pillows, he reached for the Bull Durham, began shaping another smoke, frowning slightly when recalling the way she'd stared at him soon after stepping off the stage. He struck a match, got the cigarette started. It was as if she'd recognized him . . . or thought she had. Later, in the hotel dining-room, she'd done the same, sneaking glances his way when she thought he wasn't looking. But if ever he'd seen her before, it was an incident entirely forgotten. And then he was thinking about the barman at the Jack O' Diamonds. He too had displayed some sort of recognition. And now, according to Ben Paulson, the man was dead.

* ★ ★

The front door of the boxlike house slammed shut behind the young man purporting to be Nat Anderson's son.

'You were right.' He grinned buoyantly, flopping into the nearest chair, crossing his legs, the book he'd brought with him held protectively in his lap.

Flo looked up from the newspaper she'd been reading without interest.

'About what?'

'That fellow you saw in the hotel. Seems you were right about him being dangerous. Be damned if, just a while ago, he didn't ride in with a prisoner and two dead bodies.'

Flo felt blood drain from her face, but she had no idea why.

'That's not all,' Lionel told her, enjoying the effect his news had produced. 'From what I hear, it's turning out to be a real good day for the undertaking profession.'

Still shaken by the first bit of information, Flo remained still.

'A barman from the Jack O' Diamonds,' he went on, grinning. 'Last night he got his skull bashed.' He laughed softly. 'You were right, Flo. This isn't like any town I've been in.'

★   ★   ★

Vance Beresford was poring over the Anderson papers Judge James Ogden Thackery allowed him to borrow before they were to be sent on to the county seat when, without ceremony, the door to his office was thrust open.

Until a moment ago, the passing of time had erased all fear of Frank Jelnick's having revealed anything that might jeopardize his personal security. Had he done so, that fool Paulson would already have been hammering at his door.

What stalked into his office, though, was almost as fearful.

'It was you, wasn't it?' Flo hissed, powdered face a grim, accusing mask. 'You killed him! It couldn't have been nobody else.' The deep-maroon cape draped around her shoulders lent her an even more menacing appearance.

Beresford did not move. 'Damnit, woman, keep your voice down! Then tell me what in blazes you're babbling about?'

'About Lloyd Gaynor, what else? It was you, wasn't it? You're the one who killed him?'

Very slowly, facial lines growing deep and taut, Vance Beresford refolded the pages before him, returned them to their envelope.

'Very well, since you insist. Yes, Flo, I . . . removed him. But you'll have to bear part of the responsibility for that necessity.' With sudden seething, he rose from behind the desk. 'Because you lied to me, *you bitch*! Why did you keep it from me? Why didn't you tell me you'd remarried? If that gets out it ruins everything! Every penny I've so far spent will have been wasted! You'd have no claim — '

'*I'd* have no claim? Why, you slippery

rat — you're the one who picks up the bundle. Not me. Not Lionel! What we get's no more than a handout for helping you get rich!'

On the verge of exploding, Beresford forced himself back under control.

'You ungrateful cow! Are you forgetting what you were when I found you? Nothing but an aging whore, living only two steps up from the gutter! Do you think I didn't know what you became after leaving here?' He shook his head. 'Nothing — a down-at-the-heels chippy, with not a goddamn thing to look forward to but a life on the lower streets.'

Face like chalk, the woman opened her mouth to speak, but Beresford's next onslaught slammed it shut.

'You were damn near in the gutter when I found you. It cost me money, lots of money, to make you sufficiently presentable in order to lodge a claim against Anderson's estate. It took time and money to prepare that cheap little crook posing as your son, to organize an acceptable birth certificate . . . letters to prove you'd spent a great deal of wasted effort trying to secure support from Anderson.' He broke off, took a deep breath. 'So don't you come here, acting as if you've been cheated! If it weren't for me you'd be back in some waterfront brothel, wondering where your next nickel was coming from.'

'How,' Flo asked, voice a dry, faltering rustle, 'did you know about Gaynor? He — he try to put the squeeze on you also?'

Impatiently, Beresford waved aside the question.

'It's not important, and I've no time to explain now.'

Flo left, feeling the lowest she'd ever felt in her life. Slowly descending the stairs to the street, her entire life seemed to float before her eyes, a life of erratic promise, but never any future. She'd made a lot of mistakes, especially lying to Nat Anderson when meeting him in Leadville . . . having him believe she'd been married and widowed at a young age. At the time she'd been working as a waitress at the hotel where he was staying, but before that she'd been a lot of other things.

Getting involved with Morgan Farraday was one of her biggest mistakes. That had really cost her!

She'd almost forgotten how, after leaving Cradlestone, she'd wound up in Kansas, working a saloon in Wichita. Which was where she'd met Burt — the stinking, double-crossing bastard — where she'd married him. Six months later, in some forgotten town a few hours south of Dodge, he'd ditched her. And there'd been others, until eventually, years later, she found herself in San Francisco, alone and broke and growing old.

Sheer desperation had prompted her to again write to Anderson's lawyer, but this time it had brought results.

In the form of Vance Beresford.

Reaching the street, Flo gave way to a frightened shudder. Beresford's scheme had promised opportunity and reward, and she'd leapt at it. In it now, she saw only disaster.

Slowly, like a woman twice her age, she stepped out of the corner door of the bank building, hearing nothing, seeing nothing.

Not even the tall figure under the black hat who had paused to look at her when she crossed the street, then turned back in the direction of the small house which had lately become home.

# 21

Standing at the window of his office, cursing under his breath, Beresford watched Flo cross the street. From now on much greater control over her and the runt was going to be needed. He was far too close to cashing in on his plans to allow them to become any kind of problem.

He was about to return to his desk, to get the letter to the Lane girl written, when his attention was drawn to another figure stepping into the street, and again there was that queasy sensation behind his belt. Not until Tyrell had reached the opposite side did he release his breath, and then only when realizing the man was pointed in the opposite direction. But he continued to watch, waiting until Tyrell was lost in the shadows of the covered sidewalk. He shrugged away the feeling that had started to grow. It meant nothing. There'd been no contact between him and the woman. It was no more than . . . just another coincidence, their both appearing within moments of each other.

Beresford sat down, forced himself to start the letter.

Thirty minutes later, after writing Dana Lane's name across an envelope, he rose, picked up the one containing Judge Thackery's papers, tucked both into an inside pocket, and straightened his coat. It had cost him, the preparation of those papers. The judge might have had a long-standing love affair with John Barleycorn, but if his drinking and the cost of his indulgence had made him easier to manipulate, it had yet to dull his mind. If everything went off smoothly, and there was now no reason to believe it would not, he was going to have to shell out even more to the old soak.

Unless he suffered a heart attack, or some small but fatal accident before then. Almost at the door, Vance Beresford came to a halt, surprised at how easy the idea of another killing had occurred to him.

★   ★   ★

The day was fast sinking when Tyrell pushed through the swing doors of the Jack O' Diamonds, but it was still too early for the saloon to have much of a crowd. The barkeep, a pinch-faced number, was one he'd seen before, working the other end of the long bar, assisting the apron who'd been killed. At a table close to the stairs, someone, middle aged, in an expensive suit and carrying too much weight, was dealing himself hands of solitaire while keeping a watchful eye on the bar.

Still thinking about the call he'd almost made on Beresford, Tyrell ordered a beer. It had been impulsive, based on a gut feeling strengthened by Tickner's demands for a lawyer, the discovery that Beresford had once represented Johnny DeVane, part of the 7-Bar trio, memory of Roy Henkel's dying words: *Double-crossing* . . .

He'd taken a dislike to the man when first he'd seen him at the stage depot, liked him even less when learning of the proposal he'd handed Dana — a cash settlement in compensation for her relinquishment of all claim to Cross bar A, and whatever went with it. A confrontation, though, would have achieved nothing except perhaps some personal satisfaction. Hunches, ideas, gut feelings . . . they were proof of nothing.

Wordlessly, the barkeep dumped the beer in front of him, spilling a little. Tyrell said nothing. He shoved some change across the wood, was reaching for the glass, when, a little off to his left, a voice asked bluntly:

'You Tyrell?'

He turned his head, but only slightly, and gave no reply.

'You the one stirred up trouble with that dumb-dumb — got him so riled he killed Roley Farraday?'

'My name's Tyrell. There anything else you want to know?'

'Already asked it,' the voice, heavy with confidence, snapped back. 'An' you turn around when I'm talkin' to you!'

Tyrell lifted his elbows from the wood, slowly turned. A step or two from where he'd been leaning up against the bar, two men, punchers from the looks of their worn garb, stood with thumbs hooked into gunbelts, challenging sneers pasted across broad, sun-darkened faces. Big men, heavy men — men accustomed to the power weight and size afforded them.

What little noise had been in the saloon dropped to a hush.

To the one on the right he said, 'Mister, I don't know who the hell you are, and personally I don't care if I never find out. But right now I'm tired, and in no mood for company. Especially the likes of yours. So — drift.'

'Pity you weren't so tough on Saturday — pity you had to run, leavin'

Roley to take the brunt of Hump's mad!' the second one said. Some long while ago a knife had left a deep, puckered scar across the lower left of his face.

'Yeah,' added his partner, almost a product of the same mold, except his face was the type that would always show the shadow of a beard. 'Wasn't for you, Phil would never've been forced to kill the crazy galoot.'

'Feller,' Tyrell said, 'I already told you — drift!'

'Yeah, so you did. Happens, though, we kinda like it right where we are. Maybe we can't undo what you already done to Roley, but sure's hell we can square things up a little for him.'

Tyrell turned to the barman. 'Want to call these clowns off?'

The barkeep shrugged, grinned.

'Roley Farraday was well liked around here. Had lots of friends.'

Tyrell breathed a heavy sigh. The intention was to get him whipsawed between the two of them, where he'd stand the least chance of remaining upright under the punishment they intended.

His back still to the pair, he said, 'Need to add something. I'm just too damned tired to get into a brawl of any kind. Last thing I need right now is to mess up my hands. So, boys, do me a favor and get the hell out of my way.'

With that he started what appeared to be a slow turn.

The number with the blue-shadowed jaw grinned, hunched up menacingly, and with a muttering of words totally unintelligible, dropped a shoulder and swung a right that was almost the size of a building-brick.

Stilled voices came back to life, chairs scraped against the floor when men quickly shot to their feet.

Tyrell let his body sway a little sideways, let the blow ride ineffectually across his left shoulder. By then he'd palmed his Colt. In a move, as smooth as it was fast, the barrel cracked across the side of blue-jaw's head, dropping him like a limb lightning had torn from its berth. With no hesitation of movement, the gun barrel continued its descent, until abruptly ramming itself hard into the belly of the second man. And suddenly the saloon was even quieter than it had been before.

'You want to see this through, tell me!'

Struggling to bring down his knotted fists, the man almost gagged on his own intake of breath.

'Now let's hear where you got your cockeyed information?'

Fists loosened and lifted harmlessly. As if he had sawdust in his throat, the man swallowed.

'It — it came out at the inquest. That feller Idaho — him and Scobie both told it the same way.'

Tyrell holstered his gun. 'Get them to tell it to me.'

Giving the knife-scarred man his back, he picked up his drink, swallowed half of it, thumped the glass back on the counter and left.

'Iverson!' The fleshy solitaire-player snapped. 'Don't be an even bigger damned fool!' He put down his cards, heaved his bulk from the chair he'd been occupying.

Iverson let his hand fall away from his gun.

Without being asked, the apron began pouring a double shot from the best bottle in the house.

'Not to worry.' Iverson smiled coldly. 'We'll see how high he walks after Idaho gets done with him!'

# 22

By the time she arrived home, Flo's mood had worsened. Cold and afraid, she'd never felt more in need of a drink.

Lionel was where she'd left him, slouched in the chair, nose still stuck in the book. Ignoring him, she shed her cape, went directly to the tiny kitchen and, because there was no liquor in the house, dumped the contents of the coffee-pot, rinsed and refilled it with water.

'Something wrong?'

She jerked around, found the boy standing in the doorway, clutching his book. For a while she could only stare, as if seeing him for the very first time. With that face it was hard to think of him as anything but a boy, even though he'd never see twenty-six again.

'No,' she snapped. 'Got a splitting headache, that's all.'

'Thought you said you had to pick up a few things?'

She shook her head, began measuring coffee into the enameled pot.

'Couldn't find what I wanted.'

He knew she was lying, but right then it didn't matter. He had more important matters with which to concern himself.

'Ever wonder about Beresford?' he asked, leaning his back against the door-frame. 'What his real angle is?'

Flo closed the coffee-can, returned it to the shelf.

'He told you — a profit when that damned ranch gets sold.'

'First, though, it's got to be transferred to us, right? Either you or me — or both.'

Flo put the pot on the stove, stirred up the coals and shoved in more wood.

'So?'

'When that happens we sell it to him, right? Only the price he pays is just a figure on paper. We don't get a dime — nothing more than what he promised

227

to give us. Which is chicken-feed, by comparison.' He folded his arms, pressing the book against his narrow chest. 'What I'm saying is, once the property's transferred to us, why would we still need him?'

'Forget it, kid,' she warned, avoiding his eyes. 'Friend Beresford's not someone you want to tangle with.'

Lionel smiled curiously. 'Hey . . . you're scared of him!'

'Damn right, I am!' she flared. 'Besides, get it through your head, we've got no rights to anything. Especially you. You never had any connection with Anderson.'

Letting the reprimand go on by, he brought his small frame fully upright and gave another soft chuckle.

'Never did trust that lousy shyster. Ever since he wangled us into this deal I've been wondering about his end.'

'Forget it, damnit! Don't try and get cute!'

'Why not? There's a whole hell of a lot more involved here than he's had us believe. Just think how much he must have already spent getting us fixed up and bringing us here?'

'Damnit, Lionel,' she shouted. 'I said *forget it*!'

Head slightly cocked, eyes slitted, he looked at her, kept looking until she turned away.

'All right, Flo,' he nodded. 'If that's the way you want it.'

'It is,' she snapped. 'All I want is to get everything done with, and get the hell and gone from this crummy town!'

★　★　★

Eli Cradock lay with pillow bunched up under his head, thinking of what Halyard had told him, wanting to believe it, yet not trusting the medico sufficiently to do so. Two other croakers had told him in what state his lungs were, so what the hell made this one think he knew different?

He reached for the dark bottle on the rickety table next to the bed, read the label again. It told him no more than it had the first time: how much to take, how often to take it. Mixed by the town's pharmacist, according to directions Halyard had scrawled on a square of paper, the concoction tasted like something from a mule with kidney trouble. He still wasn't sure why he'd bothered, except that he was feeling like nine kinds of hell when knocking on Halyard's door.

But, since slugging back the foul-tasting brew, and since emptying damn near half the bottle, he felt better. Still coughing, but easier now, and no longer feeling so drained. In fact, he was starting to feel hungry. He put the bottle back where it had been, lifted himself off the thin mattress, and went to the window. Other than to the sawbones and the pill-roller, he'd been nowhere.

Now he felt restless. Restless and hungry.

Shadows were thickening, slithering over roof tops. Here and there yellow lamplight was already filtering through windows, and far down the street lanterns were being lit along the boardwalk.

Sunday's cursed wind had left behind a gray, empty and depressing day. On occasion he'd watched from the solitude of the miserable room, hoping to see Tyrell, worrying that the bastard might again have put a lot of distance between them . . .

He went back to the side of the bed, uncorked the bottle, and took a double swig. As he put it down again, his eyes found the whiskey bottle. His hand reached. Stopped. Halyard had said to lay off. OK, it was a hell of a call, but he'd give it a try. For a while anyway. The now familiar warmth began flooding through his chest, and once more he wondered if the medico had not been telling him something he ought pay attention to.

Eli Cradock laughed softly, waited for his lungs to erupt into another bout of strength-sapping coughing. But it didn't happen. Still, it would be stupid, real dumb, to think the crap in that bottle was curing him. But, making him feel better . . . that he'd be a fool to deny. He laughed again, and picked up the whiskey.

From the hook behind the door he lifted his coat, shrugged into it, and put on his hat. *Damn*, but he was hungry.

*   *   *

Dana put down the letter which, only a short while ago, had been delivered by Vance Beresford's hired messenger. Once again they were seated at the table in the dining-room. She, Denver and Stretch.

'It's the same as what he told me when I saw him after church,' she said. 'Except that since then he's obtained Judge Thackery's opinion — which only supports his own.'

Denver, his left arm still cradled in a sling, snorted and expressed an opinion of his own.

'Still don't get it when he says what I got to say's got no bearin'? It's the truth! It'll show that woman up for what she is!'

'Unfortunately, it makes sense — though in a way, I think, fashioned more in the manner of law than morality.'

'Want to try that on me one more time — in English?'

Dana smiled, a smile sad, robbed of hope.

'What it means is, anything you might have to say would be regarded as prejudiced — said only to discredit her and favor my case.'

'Durned tootin' it would! Why else'd I tell it?'

Very gently she covered his unencumbered hand with one of her own, and squeezed.

'Unfortunately, in court, it would be only your word against hers. And,' she withdrew her hand, touched the letter to lend emphasis to what next she had to say, 'one fact remains irrefutable.

Uncle Nat never divorced her. In the eyes of the law she remains his legal wife, the boy his legitimate son.'

'Boiling down to what?' Stretch quietly asked.

Dana looked across the table, dampness in her eyes. 'I don't know, Stretch. I simply don't know. I've no money to contest the judge's decision — which, as Mr Beresford says, will, with little doubt, be upheld at county level.' Again her head shook, this time dislodging a tear. 'I — I just don't know.'

'I know this,' Denver proclaimed, thumping the table. 'It ain't what Nat wanted. No, sirree! — it sure as hell ain't what your uncle would've wanted had he been stoned right outa his mind! and Nat,' he added, a lot less angrily, 'was no pal of hard liquor!'

'Perhaps,' she said, voice little more than a whisper, 'it would be best to simply concede — take whatever their offer is . . . and try to find a way of making another start for ourselves.'

'No!' Again Denver thumped the

table. 'Lass, you've no idea what your uncle put into this spread. And most everythin' he done was done with you in mind.' Fixing his gaze hard upon her pallid face, he said, 'We gotta fight, girl. This whole damn thing stinks more'n a frightened polecat!'

'I agree,' Stretch Norton quietly put in, conscious and humbled by the way he had been included in the girl's suggestion of a new start. 'I liked and admired your uncle — and like Denver, I know this's not what he wanted. But where do we go from here?'

Dana brushed quickly at her eyes, picked up the letter.

'Perhaps . . . nowhere further than doing what Mr Beresford suggests.' Carefully, as if they were some sort of irreplaceable historical documents, she refolded the two pages. 'I'll see him in the morning, try to get some . . . some more advice.'

Denver Crowley gave another quiet snort before suddenly turning to Stretch.

'You told her about Roley Farraday gettin' his clock stopped?'

Dana's head came up sharply.

'Buried him this afternoon,' Stretch told the girl. 'Messenger who brought that letter told me.' He waited before going on, watching her face. 'Appears Tyrell's some way involved.'

\* \* \*

There was an air of abandonment at the house on Bent Arrow. Many had come to pay their final respects to Roley, to extend condolences to what remained of the family. A lot of them, Farraday was honest enough to admit, not because they gave a hoot in hell about either him or Phil, and particularly Roley, but only because it was good business to stay on the right side of Morgan Farraday.

Now, with everyone gone and only himself and Phil in the big front room, even the smallest sound seemed amplified.

Occupying part of his mind, too, was the damage Sunday night's wind had caused — particularly to the windmills. He carried the drink he'd poured back to his chair, stared at Phil who sat in another, arms folded, chin lolling on his chest, blind to everything except perhaps some secret mental image.

'Worried about tomorrow?' he asked, and tasted his drink. 'Got some notion Idaho won't be able to take him?'

Phil shook his head, made no comment.

'Or maybe because I've still not heard the whole story?'

'You heard,' Phil returned curtly. 'As for Idaho . . . he'll do what you're paying him to do. I've watched him practice. He's the fastest I've seen.'

'Then what the hell's gnawing at you?'

'Nothing, damnit!' Moodily, Phil heaved out of the chair. 'We buried my brother this afternoon. You forgotten that?'

'Not for a second,' Farraday told

him, tone cold and brittle. 'Which's why I'm looking forward to tomorrow — to see Idaho settle accounts.'

Yet, even as he spoke the words, Morgan Farraday kept his gaze hard upon his younger son, again wondering if he'd been told everything.

# 23

Another overcast morning had some in Cradlestone confident of rain, the less optimistic of the opinion that wind would rise up again to clear the sky and undo all that had already been put right. It had happened before, so why not now?

With other things on their minds besides the uncertain weather, six riders were headed for Cradlestone, four travelling a good half-hour ahead of the others.

Morgan and Philip Farraday rode on to the lumber yard to order timber needed for repairs; Idaho Smith and Mike Scobie veering off to Frain's stables. Dismounting, ignoring the owner when he came to take their mounts, Scobie let his reins drop and strode into the barn. Returning a minute later, he shook his head.

Watching from under shaggy grey eyebrows, Bill Frain, who missed little that went on in the valley, had a good idea what horse they were looking for. He knew both and liked neither, and so he kept silent until Idaho asked: 'When'd Tyrell leave?'

Frain squinted up at the mounted man. 'Early.'

'How early?' Idaho scowled.

Frain pretended to think about it. 'Right after breakfast.'

'Say where he was going?'

'Nope . . . and I didn't ask. His business.'

Scobie tapped the older man's chest with a stiffened finger.

'But it'd be your business to know if he was comin' back, right?'

Frain answered the question with a level look, a small sneer.

'Oh . . . no need to fret over that. He'll be back.'

Sunday's storm had left its mark across the land, as well as the town. Two hours of aimless riding revealed ample evidence of the wrath of the sudden and savage wind. Ever since leaving Cradlestone, Tyrell had been thinking of Cross bar A, hoping they'd not been too badly hit. The girl had troubles enough.

Cross bar A . . .

He reined up. On the rare occasions he'd considered a time for putting down roots, he'd pictured a place such as Nat Anderson had created . . . a woman like Dana Lane with whom to share it. He thought about it now while taking the small sack of tobacco from his pocket. Then, like thistledown caught in a breeze, the dream flew to pieces, shattered by the intrusion of reality, the smiling image of Stretch Norton moving front stage.

He lit the cigarette, the restlessness returning. He should be moving on; there was nothing for him here. But he knew he wouldn't, not until the problems confronting Dana Lane and the ranch were resolved. He already had enough incomplete memories.

After only another mile he again pulled up, this time twisting in the saddle to look back in the direction of Cradlestone, as if hearing something there calling to him. He shrugged it aside, kneed the roan again onward.

★  ★  ★

At about ten, with the town fully awake, the young man known as Lionel strolled self-assuredly along the board-walk, whistling softly when passing through the corner door of the bank building, climbing the stairs to the only occupied office on the upper floor.

Hardly was he inside when a pair of riders appeared at the east end of the broad, dusty street, loping on past the livery barn, not stopping until they reached the brick building.

'Want me to wait for you?' Norton asked.

Dana swung down to the ground.

'Not if you've something else you'd rather do.' Again she was attired in an outfit of her preference; split skirt, blouse, and half-boots. This morning, though, a fringed buckskin jacket had been added, 'I don't know how long I'll be.'

'I'll wait,' Stretch said, lifting himself out of the saddle.

Up in Vance Beresford's office, hands dug deep into the pockets of brown pants, Lionel stood smiling at the lawyer who sat with expression unbending.

'Never did trust you,' he said. 'Not from the moment you handed me that proposition.' Abruptly, his narrow face hardened. 'You lousy shyster, you've been using Flo and me to make yourself a fortune.' Rocking back on his heels, amused at Beresford's slow rise from behind the desk, he laughed softly. 'Right! I've got it. The notebook, with all its figures, drawings and calculations — everything that tells why Cross bar A's so important to certain parties. It's all there! Every beautiful thing.'

'You — lousy little bastard! — you broke into my house!' Beresford snarled, fully vertical now, in his face a rising fury struggling against control, a danger Lionel failed to recognize.

'As it turned out,' he shrugged, 'a very easy task. Actually,' he went on, smugly reviving the smile, 'all I was looking for was something that might tell me more about you and your scheme. Instead, I found the — what do miners call it? — the mother lode?' He laughed softly. 'What we need now to discuss, my friend, is a better deal. A much, much better deal. Because if what's in that book was made public . . . Well, I don't think the Farradays would be too happy. It'd also blow your scheme to hell, wouldn't it?'

'Why, you lousy little . . . ' Too furious to finish, Beresford sucked in his breath, still struggling to maintain restraint. 'If it weren't for me you could be wearing a prison suit instead of that fancy outfit. You were nothing but a cheap little crook when steered to me. A lousy, now-and-again actor — a pimp — a third-rate thief!'

The younger man held his easy smile. 'Who now happens to be in control of the situation.'

Beresford continued to glare, the color of his face dangerously darkening, the words thrown at him adding fuel to the anger tightening the muscles in his throat.

Lionel moved closer to one of the two padded chairs between which he stood, prepared to sit, but before the move was half-way complete Beresford was around the desk, huge hands fastening around his throat.

'You filthy piece of scum!' he hissed through bared teeth. 'Where is it? What've you done with it?'

Lionel clawed at powerful wrists, feeling himself lifted off his feet, pressure building up behind his eyes. Only vaguely aware of what he was doing he reached under his coat for the pocket Colt.

'Where is it?' Beresford asked again, louder, angrier.

Something began to nudge his breastbone. He stiffened, dropped his left from the boy's throat, made a frantic grab, huge hand almost completely encasing Lionel's, twisting it away from his own body, squeezing.

Under the pressure, Lionel's grip on the small gun closed tight. Adding to his terror as he struggled to breathe was the knowledge that the gun was designed without a trigger guard, that the increasing pressure around his hand was forcing the trigger backward . . .

Dana was almost at the office door when she heard Beresford's loud, demanding voice. Hand upon the doorknob, she came up short at the sound of a muffled explosion, another following like a delayed echo.

'Mr Beresford — ?' She thrust open the door.

Beresford whirled, letting go of the thing still held tightly by its throat, letting it drop like an old and badly used rag doll. She saw the gun almost lost in his huge fist when he turned to face her, eyes showing more white than ever.

As sudden as the wind that had lashed at him on Sunday night, in the girl's horrified expression he saw ruin and defeat staring at him . . . every single thing he'd planned, so carefully put together, come crumbling down. And all because of a miserable piece of dirt like that which lay at his feet . . . because of the foolish woman who stood gaping at him as if he were some kind of monster.

'Dana . . . Listen . . . This isn't . . . '

Before the last word left his lips the girl had turned, and already he could hear her boots clattering down the stairs. He shouted for her to stop, knowing she wouldn't . . . knowing he had to prevent her from raising an alarm. Perhaps . . . perhaps there was still a way to cover up what had happened. With such thoughts rattling through his head he went after her, long, sturdy legs taking the steps four at a time, grabbing her just as she was pulling open the street door.

Dana screamed when the hand clamped on her shoulder, jerking her half-way round. Fear stood naked in Beresford's eyes.

'Wait!' he panted. 'Dana — wait!'

She heard his words at the same time as something hard was dug into her ribs.

At the hitch rack, Norton, startled by the sudden skirmish at the bank-building door, flung aside his smoke, grabbed for his pistol, yelled at the heavy figure holding on to the girl. He yelled again, unaware of the screams of people who had stopped to stare.

Vaguely, Vance Beresford wondered where he was going, what had happened. For the first time in his life he knew absolute confusion. But instinct for survival remained dominant. Shoving the girl aside he brought the gun to bear on Norton. He heard her scream again, saw nothing of the quick shift of

Norton's eyes, only the gun pointing at him . . .

Stretch's gaze flashed back to the gray-suited man, saw his face stiffen, terror rob it of still more color . . . felt something hard punch into his left thigh, not powerful enough to knock him over, but to send him back a couple of steps. He brought up the .44, tried to locate Beresford, but the man was already mounting the boardwalk of the next block, shouldering aside all who were in his way.

# 24

Cutting the straightest trail he could manage back to Cradlestone, Tyrell reached the town still not knowing what it was that had drawn him back.

As he entered the main street his gaze raked the wide drag and caught some kind of commotion near the bank. Touching heels to the big gelding, he continued on at a quick lope, trying to make sense of the shouting. On his left, but three blocks from the bank, he saw people hastily deserting the sidewalk. Marshal Paulson appeared on the street, running toward the red-brick building.

Someone was on the ground, a few crouched around whoever it was. Robbery was the first and most natural thought that came to mind, until one of the crouched figures rose, talking urgently, and at sight of her

Tyrell's heart plunged.

As though his fear had become a tangible thing that reached out to touch her, Dana Lane turned, saw him about to lift the roan to a faster pace, and as quickly swung her gaze to the board-walk leading away from the bank. He saw her mouth open, knew she was either shouting or calling, but could hear nothing, for the shouts had become louder, as had the thumping of heavy boots hurrying along the planks.

Their high-pitched screams drowning every other sound, two women left the shaded boardwalk. Then a larger, heavier figure lunged on to the street, paused briefly as if trying to figure where to go — then saw the rider descending upon him. Eyes bulging, face twisted in an ugly grimace, he brought the small gun up, cursing when recognizing Tyrell . . . oddly conscious that things had started to fall out of line only after he'd shown up in Cradle-stone.

The roan was almost upon him when

Beresford fired. He knew he'd hit something, knew also that Tyrell was leaving leather — not falling, but throwing his full weight at him.

He hit the ground on his back, air blasting from his lungs, mind whirling in a mixture of hate and fury, of fear and the bitterness of defeat. He saw Tyrell rising, blood on his arm . . . realized he was still gripping the gun, and let his hand fist up.

Screaming when from nowhere the hard toe of a boot smashed into his thick fingers and sent the gun spinning, he forced himself to his feet, face dark, a distorted smear of maddened rage when finding Tyrell standing, nodding slowly, knowingly.

'I should have had you killed the moment you rode into the valley!' he snarled, hands twisting into thick claws.

'Same as you had Nat Anderson killed?'

Beresford's reply was little more than an animal sound when charging his accuser. But Tyrell was waiting, and in him there was also anger, but of a different kind. Still ignorant of what had happened at the bank, what Dana's part in it was, knowing only that the man before him was in some way involved, his first blow caught the lawyer square in the face, and under the second he felt something crunch and give away. After that, it was like looking at Beresford through a scarlet haze, until hands pulled at him, forcing his arms down.

There was blood in his mouth, a searing burn in his upper left arm, a deeper ache in ribs that had already been badly punished. Dimly, he heard Paulson's voice.

'Easy, feller, easy!'

He let his arms relax, looked down at where Beresford lay unmoving, a large crumpled mass of gray.

'What happened? Dana — she all right?'

Paulson gave a few sharp orders, then started steering him away.

'He shot the kid — the one claiming

to be Anderson's son.'

'Dead?'

'Never be any deader.' He wheeled Tyrell about. 'C'mon, let's get that arm looked at, even if it is just a scratch.'

'Miss Lane . . . ?'

'She's OK. Matter of fact, that's her coming our way now. Norton, though, he's going to be joining old Denver, resting up a while.' The marshal stopped, still holding on to Tyrell. 'Never noticed till only just now . . . until Norton got hit. She . . . '

'Yeah,' Tyrell said quietly, watching the girl hurrying to them.

★   ★   ★

Leaving Doc Halyard, Tyrell started down the street, headed for the hotel. Paulson had let the girl take him to be patched up, returning to his own duties, promising to see that the roan was taken to the livery barn.

He'd lingered at the medico's, offering what help he could in getting

254

Stretch Norton loaded into a buggy Bill Frain had made available.

When it was done, Dana had turned to him.

'Please come out to the ranch as soon as you're able. There — there's still so much I don't understand . . .'

A while later he'd watched her and Norton drive out of town, their horses hitched to the rear of the vehicle, continuing to watch until they were lost from sight.

Two blocks from the hotel, a section of town where activity was usually the greatest, he heard his name called.

'You hear me?' Idaho called again.

Knowing what waited for him, he stopped, slowly turned.

Poised in the middle of the street, relishing the way people backed off to safety, the manner in which women grabbed small children, shoving them through the doorways of the nearest stores, confidence curved Smith's long upper lip into a lopsided smile. What had happened down at the bank would be nothing compared to what they were about to see. The sound of his voice had brought Cradlestone to a virtual standstill, diverting attention until it was centered entirely upon himself, standing with boots carefully spaced apart, right hand dangling near his cut-away holster.

Tyrell stepped off the sidewalk, narrowing his gaze.

Always he'd known that this moment would inevitably arrive. Since their first encounter Smith had showed signs of wanting to prove himself better, though for what purpose, Tyrell could only guess. Until their most recent meeting, however, Idaho had been careful not to force a confrontation. But perhaps until now no one had paid a high enough price for his gun.

'You hear me, Webb?'

'Would be hard not to.'

'Know why I'm here?'

'Guess you'd better tell me.'

'To settle for a friend,' Smith

returned, spacing his words, making sure none of those trapped as unwilling spectators on both sidewalks would miss a syllable.

Making no reply, and without moving his head, Tyrell let his gaze skim the street, sweeping windows and rooftops for hidden guns. Over to his left, standing close to the edge of the boardwalk, were Morgan Farraday, his one-eyed son, and the smirking Scobie.

Farraday stood stone-faced, his interest no longer fully focused on this thing he'd engineered, this killing he'd looked forward to witnessing. Ever since watching the battered and bleeding lawyer hauled off to the calaboose there'd been the feeling of trouble pressing in around him. His interest in securing Cross bar A was the only thing that could link him to Beresford. But if that damned geologist's notebook was found . . .

Idaho Smith's voice brought his attention back to the street.

'I'm talking about Roley Farraday, Webb . . . about you being responsible for his death.'

A brief sigh slipped across Tyrell's lips. Now he had a better understanding of what this was all about.

'Better explain that.'

'Be a pleasure,' Idaho smiled, voice maintaining its careful pitch. 'Wasn't for you stirring up that idiot Sinden, getting him so all-fired mad, Roley'd still be alive. Wasn't for your big mouth, your needling of the dimwit, Phil would never've had any reason to shoot the poor devil. Way I see it,' he continued, aware that he'd captured an audience large enough to satisfy the demands of Morgan Farraday, 'you're to blame for all that happened. Every damned thing.'

'Hold it!' another voice bellowed from behind where Idaho stood. 'There'll be no gunplay on this street — or any street. We've had enough trouble for one day.'

'Keep out of this, Paulson,' Farraday

snapped. 'This is personal.'

'Farraday, I'm not telling you again — '

'And I won't repeat myself! You want to go on wearing that badge — keep your nose out of this.'

'Move back, Marshal,' Tyrell called. 'This day's been a long time coming.' *And, he thought, it had to be this day . . . this particular time.* To the smiling Idaho he said, 'If you've run out of wind, it OK for me to say something?'

Fingers flexing close to the butt of his Colt, Smith smiled a little more broadly, aware that after what they'd done to Beresford, Tyrell's hands wouldn't be in the best shape to handle a gun.

'Be my guest.'

'You're a liar, Idaho. But then, most times, you and the truth have been strangers.'

Smith blanched, right hand dipped fractionally, but he froze the motion.

'Nobody calls me that and lives!'

'You're a liar, Idaho. A dirty, stinking liar.'

The accusation washed the smile from the gunman's face, had his waiting hand sweeping, snatching, the Colt leaving leather smooth and fast, just as he knew it would, perhaps even faster than at any time during the many hours of practice. He felt the hammer slide smoothly back under his thumb, the barrel tipping, lining up on its target. With the feel of his forefinger tightening, the sound of a blast echoing along the street, the smile returned.

For a moment.

Then, as if everything was happening within the span of a lightning flash, there came the realization that only then had the gun bucked in his grasp — that a blow to his chest was driving him into a couple of stiff retreating steps.

Mouth agape, he stared through the smoke drifting from Tyrell's gun, saw the man looking back at him without the slightest expression. Idaho tried to curse, but the words he managed were no more than a gurgle. He righted himself, braced his legs, forced his hand to lift, to steady the gun . . .

Tyrell waited, his own weapon ready to respond. Smith fired, but the shot was off by a foot. He tried once more, but the gun was becoming an impossible weight. He let his arm sag, his legs fold, saw the image of Webb Tyrell swallowed up in a darkening fog.

From where the Farradays watched, Mike Scobie let rip a sharp curse, grabbed for his gun, but jerked his hand quickly away when hearing Paulson's sharp warning, seeing the lawman's gun levelled at him.

Paulson shouted again, fired a warning shot, this time at Phil Farraday. Tyrell moved his head, saw the hand drop from the gun butt. He swung his gaze back to Scobie, left hand fingering his neck, checking the blood on his fingers. Just a little closer and it would have been Idaho's day . . .

Holstering the Colt, he moved closer

to where Scobie and the Farradays stood.

'Any time you want, Scobie.' His gaze swung to Phil. 'Same goes for you. Any time you want.'

'Tyrell,' Paulson shouted. 'It's over!'

'Not yet, Marshal. Not yet.' Now he was looking only at Scobie. 'I'll wait only three seconds more.'

'Paulson!' the older Farraday said loud, but with a hollowness that echoed in his ears. 'You'd better stop this.'

'Three seconds,' Tyrell repeated before Paulson could respond to the demand. 'Or you tell it, loud and clear, what happened out at Bent Arrow on Saturday.'

'Marshal!'

'Quiet!' Paulson growled. 'This could be something we might all like to hear.'

'All right!' Scobie screamed, sidling away from Farraday's son. 'All right! It was Phil! He — '

'Shut up, you damned fool!' Phil made a grab for him.

'Leave him!' his father rasped. 'Let

him talk.' He nodded for Scobie to continue.

'It — it was Phil who started it,' Scobie whined, looking as if he'd never smile again. 'Made Hump beat up on — on him!' He shoved a shaking finger toward Tyrell. 'Afterwards — after he was gone, Roley started slapping the big ape around. Hump got mad. Hit him — an' Phil — Phil shot him.'

Morgan Farraday listened, making no attempt to interrupt until Scobie was through talking. Then, heavy shoulders slumped, he looked at his son, started to ask a question, and lost the need when seeing Phil's ashen face.

Turning, walking back to the saloon, the planked walk felt like quicksand under his boots.

# 25

For the rest of the afternoon Marshal Ben Paulson had his hands more than full, most of the time trying to get responses to questions still needing answers. Beresford, though, remained tight-lipped, his battered face sullen, his legal mind advocating extreme caution while searching for a loophole through which to crawl and escape the mess he was in.

Only when locked in the cell adjoining Len Tickner's, with Paulson and two witnesses standing by, with the small, frightened man showing every readiness to talk his head off if it would save his own skin, did the lawyer start to crack.

When the woman called Flo was brought in, the crack opened wide.

Later, over a drink in the saloon, Paulson filled Tyrell in. Putting down his empty glass, signalling for refills, he squinted up at the taller man.

'Everything's about cleared up. What's left won't be too tough to handle. But you . . . I'm still finding it hard to get your number.'

Tyrell shrugged, and was saved from having to answer by an overweight figure looming up behind them.

'Marshal,' he smiled, dropping a pudgy hand on Paulson's shoulder, 'I believe congratulations are in order. Quite a job you've done.'

As if given some secret sign, the pinch-faced apron was there to receive orders. 'Tonight,' said the fat man, 'the money of these two gentlemen is of no use in the Jack O' Diamonds.'

Still later, after eating at the hotel, and with his thoughts at Cross bar A, Tyrell walked to the livery stable, wanting to arrange something with Bill Frain. Except for two lanterns glowing a welcome above the wide door, the dark around the building was complete. He stepped into the spill of light, was almost at the door, when, from the dark a voice rasped:

'Far as you go, Tyrell!'

Warily, he turned.

At the rim of the light-pool, tall and gaunt, a man with glacier-cold eyes, who looked to be well past middle age, yet wasn't, stood with bony hand clutching a Walker .44.

'Remember me?'

'Not offhand.' Tyrell straightened, narrowing his gaze.

'The name Cradock help?' The voice was harsh, whispery, like sand sifting across a tin roof. 'Jonah and Abel Cradock?'

It came back then, the memory of a night in Nogales . . .

He'd entered the saloon minutes after the marshal had been gunned down when attempting to arrest three drunken hardcases who'd been shooting up the place. Thinking him to be a deputy, they'd turned their guns on him as soon as he shoved through the batwings. When the smoke cleared, two of the trio lay dead. The third, the tallest, let his gun hit the sawdust.

Once they'd been the feared Cradock brothers, who'd established a bloody reputation throughout the Nations, later shifting their activities down to New Mexico. But that fact became known to Webb Tyrell only after the remaining brother had been tossed in the slammer.

He studied the man poised before him. When arrested, Eli Cradock, the oldest of the brothers, had not yet turned forty.

'Barely recognized you, Eli.'

Cradock nodded. 'Six years in Yuma'll do that to a man. Got myself the prison plague whils' in that stinkin' hell-hole. And damn near one o' them night-time burials. But I fooled 'em, Tyrell. My lungs might be rotted, but I'm here now — set on doin' what I been waitin' six stinkin' years to do. That's all that kept me goin', Tyrell — the thought of settlin' with you for what you did to my brothers. Took a while to find you . . . always you were a day or three ahead of me. But I found you, just like I always knew I'd do.'

'You're a free man again, Cradock. Why spoil it?'

'I'm a dead man,' Cradock wheezed. 'A dead man that's gonna send you to hell a while before he makes the ride.' The last word was still being spoken, when the gun in his hand made a small forward thrust.

Then, just as his forefinger began squeezing, Cradock's chest tightened, heaved, and threw throttling phlegm up into his throat. He froze, choking and, despite the desperate effort made to quell the cough building up like a cyclone in his lungs, Eli Cradock doubled over, hacking violently, incapable of holding one position.

On the verge of triggering the drawn Colt, Tyrell locked a thumb on the hammer.

What seemed a long while later, the gaunt man's body relaxed. He spat at the ground and, chest heaving, tried to pull himself upright, free hand fishing for his handkerchief. In his right the gun hung heavily.

'Ride out, Eli,' Tyrell said quietly. 'Make the best of what days you've still got. There could still be plenty.' He slid the gun between leather, turned toward the partly-open door of the livery.

'We're not through, you bastard!' Cradock wheezed.

Tyrell stopped, sighing wearily.

'I came to kill you, and that's exactly what I aim to do!' The Walker was already lifting, lining up on its target's back.

In a single movement Tyrell dropped into crouch, stepped to the right, and heeled sharply about.

Whether or not he heard his own shot was something Eli Cradock would never tell, for after taking three stumbling backward steps, he became motionless, staring with all the hate and disappointment he could summon.

'Son . . . of a . . . bitch,' he muttered,

and a moment later there was a new face in hell.

* ★ ★ ★

'Reckon that's about everything,' Ben Paulson said, winding up his report. 'Nothing but a scheme put together by Beresford to get control of Cross bar A, using what he knew about the underground reservoir to eventually grab the valley itself.'

It was later afternoon, and with what remained of her crew, Denver still carrying an arm in a sling; Norton sitting with his injured leg stretched poker-straight, they were gathered on the gallery of the ranch house.

'Told you!' Denver snorted. 'That danged woman never was no good. Never figured her to be the mother of anybody's kid, 'specially Nat's!'

Dana leaned forward, a small frown on her brow, 'Was Morgan Farraday involved?'

'Indirectly, yes. Like getting your

270

crew scared off. Mostly, though, I think, he was just another sucker in Beresford's scheme.'

'He's confessed?' Dana asked.

'Not willingly, but we've got him cold on the boy's killing, also Gaynor's — the barkeep. The rest'll take some time to get sorted out — like proving letters that were supposed to've been written by Flo Anderson were forgeries he'd organized. Meantime, I've talked with Judge Thackery — who, I think, himself has a few things to explain. Right now, though, he can't find a single reason why your uncle's will can't be executed, just like he wanted.'

Stretch stirred uncomfortably. 'The boy — you find out who he was?'

'According to the woman, his name was Lionel Stolz — a petty crook whom Beresford recruited.' Ben Paulson rose, picking his hat up from the floor as he did, glancing from Norton to Dana, feeling a little envy, a little more than disappointment. 'As for her . . . your uncle may never have divorced her, but

271

the fact that she married again . . . that puts an end to a lot of things. Meanwhile, she's singing like a canary with its tail feathers on fire.'

Dana lowered her eyes. 'In spite of everything . . . I feel sorry for her.'

'Don't, girl,' Denver cautioned. 'You don't know her.'

'Still . . . ' She let it go, and stood up, again frowning. 'I — I rather expected to see Mr Tyrell out here today . . . '

Paulson fiddled with his hat. 'There was some trouble last night, at the livery — after he killed Smith, got Scobie to open up about what really happened at Bent Arrow.' He gave them the details in just a few words, wrapping it up by fitting his hat to his head. 'Bill Frain was on hand to see and hear everything. Swears Tyrell had no choice in the matter. Fact of the matter is, all the time he was listening, he had a rifle lined on Cradock, ready to blast him away if Tyrell missed.'

Conscious of the silence from those who'd been listening, Paulson said in a much quieter voice, 'This morning I stopped at the hotel to talk with him. But he wasn't there. Told he checked out a while before daybreak.'

Dana's frown deepened. 'Checked out . . . ?

'He's gone,' Paulson said. ''Paid Bill Frain what he was owed, saddled up, and . . . well, he's gone, Dana.'

'Reckon he wanted it like that, Missy. Quiet, no fuss.'

Stretch turned to where the sun was getting ready to hide itself behind the hills. Slowly he brought his gaze to the old man.

'Think he might be on the dodge?'

Denver shook his head, remembering what Tyrell had said about everyone probably running from something.

'Could be. But . . . personally, I kinda doubt it. Had to make a guess, I'd say, more'n likely he's lookin' for somethin'.'

Dana was now also faced in the same direction as the others. 'Looking . . . for what?' she asked, and of no one but herself.

Barely moving his head, Denver slid his gaze upon the girl. *Not sure, lass. Might be . . . might be for a while he found it.*

Struggling to his feet, jerking his battered old hat down tighter upon his head, he said, 'Reckon only he knows that.'

## THE END